While Persephone yakked away about Zeus and Hera's wedding, I ate my way through her picnic. I was just wondering whether it would be rude to ask if there were any more ambrosia potato salad, when I heard a faint *zing!* Then I felt a sudden sharp sting on the back of my neck.

"Ow!" I cried, slapping my neck. Had a bee stung me?

"What's wrong, Hades?" asked Persephone. "Did you swallow a bone?"

Cerberus started circling me, whimpering.

I felt around on my neck. There was a little sticky ichor (old Greek-speak for "god blood"). Then I felt something poking into my flesh. Something prickly. I yanked it out. It was a tiny golden arrow. Where had that come from?

"Hades?" Persephone was saying. "Hades? Are you all right?"

Her voice sounded far away.

I blinked and managed to focus again. I looked at Persephone. And that's when it hit me like a ton of ambrosia potato salad. Persephone was the most beautiful, the kindest, loveliest, most adorable goddess I'd ever laid eyes on.

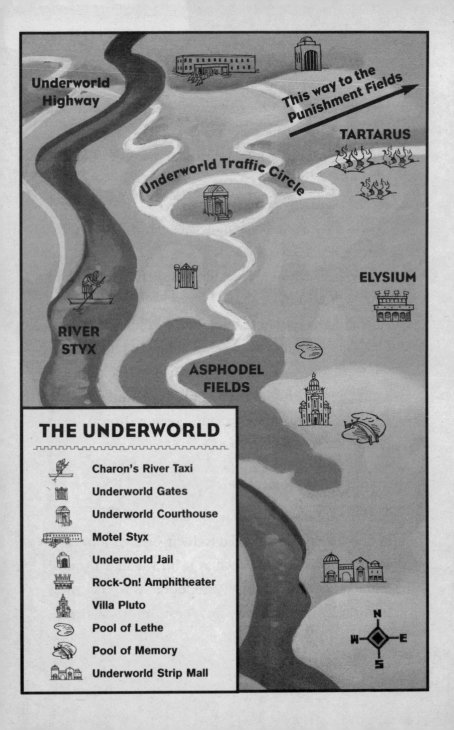

Phone Home, PERSEPHONE!

By
Kate McMullan

Illustrated by
David LaFleur

SCHOLASTIC INC.

New York Toronto London Auckland Sydney
Mexico City New Delhi Hong Kong Buenos Aires

For Leigh,
who always remembers to phone home

ЛЛЛЛЛЛЛ

Eternal libations for
my muse-editor, Susan Chang,
and my agent, Holly McGoddess

ISBN 0-439-43049-6

Text copyright © 2002 by Kate McMullan.
Illustrations copyright © 2002 by David LaFleur. All rights reserved.
Published by Scholastic Inc., 557 Broadway, New York, NY 10012,
by arrangement with Hyperion Books for Children, an imprint of
Disney Children's Book Group, LLC. SCHOLASTIC and associated
logos are trademarks and/or registered trademarks of Scholastic Inc.

12 11 10 9 8 7 6 5 4 3 2   3 4 5 6 7/0

Printed in the U.S.A.   40

First Scholastic printing, December 2002

Prologue

It's me again, Hades. You know, Lord of the Dead? Ruler of the Underworld? Right. That Hades.

If you've read any of the Greek myths, then you know that my little brother, Zeus, is Ruler of the Universe. But did you know that Zeus is also the Biggest Liar in the Universe? He lies about his weight. He lies about his height. He even lies about his sandal size. He is a total myth-o-maniac (old Greek-speak for "big fat liar"). So is it any surprise that Zeus's version of the myths is a pack of lies?

Take *The Big Fat Book of Greek Myths*, for example, the latest selection from the Big-Fat-Book-

of-the-Month Club. The stories are all about mighty, monster-slaying Zeus. Powerful, thunderbolt-hurling Zeus. Handsome, irresistible-to-goddesses Zeus. Zeus is always the hero. And who is eternally cast in the role of the bad guy? The sulky, bad-tempered brother, banished to the Underworld? Three guesses: Hades, Hades, Hades.

Just take a look at what Zeus did to the story of how I met my bride, Persephone. I swear, he made the whole thing up just to make me look bad. Go on, read it for yourself!

One day Persephone, the goddess of spring, was picking flowers. Suddenly, the earth split open. Up from its depths sprang Hades, King of the Underworld! He whipped his steeds toward Persephone, grabbed the maiden, and drove back into the earth, which sealed up behind him.

Total poppycock! Persephone wasn't out picking any flowers. She was running away from her overprotective mother. And I never grabbed her. She hitched a ride to the Underworld!

I couldn't stand it that everyone who read the myths would think of me as some sort of kidnapper. That's why I wrote my own book—to tell the world the truth. So here's the real deal on how I met Persephone, and how she became part-time Queen of the Underworld.

Chapter I

DIAL-A-GODDESS

A few millennia ago, we gods defeated our big bad dad, Cronus, and his Titan brothers in a colossal battle for control of the cosmos. After we won the war, we had to decide who would be the new Ruler of the Universe. I was all set to take over. I was the oldest god, for one thing. Plus, I knew I was strong enough, brave enough, and smart enough to be top god.

But my sneaky little brother, Zeus, had other ideas. He convinced us—my sisters Hestia, Demeter, and Hera, my brother Poseidon, and me—to settle the question by playing a game of poker. Who won?

Zeus, of course, with a little help from some extra aces up his sleeve. He took over Dad's old job as Ruler of the Universe. After a lot of quarreling, Hestia became goddess of the hearth, Demeter became goddess of agriculture, Hera became goddess of marriage, and Poseidon became god of the seas.

Even before things got sorted out, I'd had it with my squabbling siblings. I was so sick of them all that I volunteered to move down to the Underworld, and become its king.

For me, the Underworld was perfect. My brothers and sisters would never visit me, because they'd have to walk for days and days to get here. It was the only place in the universe that gods couldn't simply chant the astro-traveling spell and—*ZIP!*—show up. The Underworld was private. It was quiet. It was home.

But every once in a while, I needed a change of scene. One thing I liked to do was hitch my steeds, Harley and Davidson, to my chariot and gallop up to earth to catch a wrestling match. The mortals in Athens, a city in Greece, were wild about wrestling in those days. Since I'd competed in wrestling in the very first Olympic Games, the Athenians treated me like a champ. They even gave me free seats in their new wrestling stadium, fourth-row center.

One day, I saw a great match between "Eagle Eye" Cyclops and "Hot Mouth" Chimera. I had three uncles who were Cyclopes, and I always rooted for their wrestling relatives. I put my money on Eagle Eye, who defeated the fire-breathing Chimera. I won a bundle. Afterward, I left the stadium, tipped the valet-parking mortal, jumped into my chariot, and took off down the main street of Athens.

It had changed quite a bit over the last few hundred years. Where once there had been only a few goat-cheese and fig stands, now enterprising mortals had set up new shops: Demetri's Sandal Repair, Sea-Nymph Bait and Tackle, and even Ari's Speedy Wedding Chapel, with a sign that read: GOT X MINUTES? GET MARRIED HERE! Why anyone would want to do such a thing, I had no idea. My brother Zeus had been married seven times and counting. But me? I was absolutely and completely happy as a single god.

I rode out of Athens and cut through a field, heading for the cave that's my secret shortcut entrance to the Underworld. Not far from the mouth of the cave, I saw someone waving wildly at me. She wasn't very big, so at first I thought she was a mortal. But as I drew closer, I saw that she had the telltale glow all immortals have, and I realized my mistake.

"Whoa, Harley! Whoa, Davidson!" I called, pulling on the reins.

My steeds slowed down and came to a halt beside the goddess. I'd never seen her before, but that was hardly surprising. My brothers and sisters and the other Olympians were always marrying each other and having children. You mortals might think that's strange, but from the beginning of time, we immortals have always married each other. The truth is, we gods live by different rules from you humans.

In any case, I didn't get up to Mount Olympus much, so there were lots of gods and goddesses I hadn't ever met. This goddess had long, honey-colored hair pulled back in a flowered headband.

Her white robe was belted with a flowered girdle (old-speak for "belt"). She even had a little flower-print purse and matching sandals. Over one arm she carried a big picnic basket.

"Hi!" the goddess said. "Oh, what fine steeds!"

She ran over and began patting my horses, and I noticed that wherever her feet touched the earth, pink clover sprang forth on the spot. Harley and Davidson noticed this, too, and right away they started nibbling.

"May I help you in some way?" I asked, stepping out of my chariot.

The goddess nodded. "Can you give me a lift?" she asked. "I mean, you don't have to, if it's too much trouble, but I really do need a ride."

"Okay," I said. "I hope it isn't too far, though, because I have to get back to the Underworld and walk my dog."

"The Underworld?" The goddess gasped and stepped closer to me. She smelled just like a flower herself. "You live in the Underworld?"

I nodded. "I'm Hades. I rule the place. And you are . . . ?"

"Oh!" The goddess clasped her hands together. "I've never met anyone who's actually been to the Underworld, and now here I am, meeting the king! I am *so* excited. I'm Persephone, by the way, goddess of spring. Maybe you've heard of me?"

I hadn't, but it seemed rude to say so. Before I could say anything, a loud ringing filled the air.

Persephone reached into her purse and pulled out the tiniest little telephone I'd ever seen. She held it to her ear. "Hello?" she said sweetly. Then she sighed and said, "What now, Mom?"

Persephone listened as her mother talked for several minutes. She looked at me, and rolled her eyes. Every once in a while, she said, "Uh-huh. Uh-huh." At last she said, "I'm fine! You have to stop calling me every two minutes! Really, Mom. I can't take it anymore. I'll call you later." She hit a button on the phone. "Ohhhhh! Why can't Mom see that I'm a grown goddess now? I don't need her hovering over me every second!"

"Right," I said. "Can I see your phone?" We gods had invented all sorts of cool gadgets thousands of years before you mortals ever thought of them, but I'd never seen a little phone like Persephone's. Where were the cords? The plugs? The wires?

Persephone tossed it to me. It was made of shiny brass. A little copper rod stuck out of its top. But that was it. No wires.

"How does it work?" I asked.

"Who knows?" Persephone shrugged. "It's my purse phone. Mom invented it to keep tabs on me." She sighed. "I'd like to toss it off a cliff, but Mom would just think up something even *worse* to keep track of me."

I gave the phone back and Persephone slipped it into her purse.

"Well, if you still need that ride . . ." I said.

"I have a better idea." Persephone's eyes sparkled. "I'd love to see the Underworld. How about taking me down and giving me a tour?"

"Can't do it," I said. "No visitors are allowed in the Underworld."

Persephone pulled a jar out of her picnic basket. She popped off the top and held it out to me. Mmmmm. Something smelled divine.

"Pretty please?" Persephone said. "With ambrosia dill pickles on top?"

I stared at that pickle jar. I was ready for a little ambrosia pick-me-up. We gods need to eat ambrosia and drink nectar pretty regularly to boost our immortality. Oh, we'd still live forever without them, but we'd look all shrunken and withered. By themselves, ambrosia and nectar are very sweet, but tasty mortal food laced with a dollop of ambrosia? Yum! I was ready to make the deal.

Harley whinnied then, and the sound brought me back to my senses.

"Not even for a pickle," I told her. "Impossible." I watched sadly as the jar disappeared back into the picnic basket.

"But why?" asked Persephone. "I mean, just for a quick little visit?" She began wheedling and pacing, and more pink clover sprang up beneath her footsteps. "Oh, come on, Hades. I've heard about the mysterious Underworld forever, but no one I know has seen it. It would be so cool if I could be the first one to take a peek!"

I shook my head.

"Why not?" Persephone asked.

"The only ones who can enter my kingdom easily are the ghosts of dead mortals," I explained. "I have this guard dog, Cerberus. He'd rip a living mortal to pieces if one tried to get through the Gates of the Underworld. He might do the same to a god or goddess," I added to discourage her. "But I don't know for sure, because they'd have to hike for nine days and nine nights to get to my kingdom, and the Olympians aren't exactly into hiking."

Persephone put her hands on her hips. "Are you trying to tell me that it takes *you* nine days and nights to get home?"

"Not me," I admitted. "I know a shortcut."

"Are you the only one who knows it?"

Persephone sure asked a lot of questions. But I figured there was no harm in answering this one.

"No," I said. "Hermes guides the ghosts of the dead down to the Underworld, so I let him in on it, too."

"But what happens when you give a party?" Persephone asked.

"A party!" I exclaimed. "I never give parties! Ever!"

Persephone seemed to light up. "An Underworld party!" she exclaimed. "Now, *that* is a great idea!"

The very thought of a party in my kingdom made me shudder. Gods and goddesses showing up and sloshing nectar punch all over my palace. Loud music. Dancing. *Ugh!*

Suddenly, Persephone's phone rang again. Her smile faded as she groped in her purse.

"Is that your mom?" I asked, happy to change the subject.

"Probably," Persephone answered grimly. "Of course Mom didn't let me get caller ID, so I never know for sure." She put the phone to her ear. "Hello?"

The expression on her face told me that it was her mom.

Persephone was pretty cute, as goddesses go, but I had to get back to my duties in the Underworld. Cerberus would be wondering where I was, and my staff would be expecting me to make my usual rounds of the kingdom. It was time for me to get going. I wasn't worried about not giving Persephone a ride. She was a goddess, after all, and could astro-travel anywhere she wanted to go.

I wished I'd thought to bring my Helmet of Darkness with me. When I put it on—*POOF!* I'm invisible. Me, and anything I'm carrying. It would have been a dramatic way to make my exit. But I didn't have the helmet, so I mouthed, "Gotta go!" and waved to Persephone. She waved back and kept talking into her purse phone. I jumped into my chariot, picked up the reins, and gave a gentle tap to my steeds. (That's another lie from my myth-o-maniac brother, Zeus. I *never* whip my steeds!) Off they galloped.

It doesn't take me nine days and nine nights to get home. But still, it's a long, hard trip down steep slopes, around scary curves and hairpin turns. It's an exciting ride, but it can wear a god out.

As I steered Harley and Davidson down the course, I could still smell the scent of clover. I thought how nice it would be if we had a patch of clover in the Underworld. I made a mental note to speak to my gardener, Cal.

At last I reached the bank of the River Styx, the fearsome Underworld river. Its dark, swirling waters may seem frightening to some, but to me, they are the waters of home. I looked up the river. Charon's River Taxi was headed my way. It's a crazy ferryboat, pieced together out of odd bits of wood and metal. Charon's pretty crazy-looking, too, with his wild white hair and his long white beard.

"Ahoy!" called Charon. He gave a final push with his pole and nosed his boat onto the bank. Then he launched into his one and only speech. "That'll be one gold coin per passenger," he said. "Living gods, hand the coin directly to me. Dead, mortals, have a relative slip it under your tongue."

As if he couldn't see who I was! I hopped out of my chariot and led my steeds onto his boat. Aside from his standard speech, Charon wasn't much of a talker. He poled silently across the river. At last the bow of the ferry touched the far shore. I led Harley and Davidson off the boat, dropping the usual gold coin into Charon's greedy palm as I went.

"I'll need another one of those, Lord Hades," said Charon.

"What?" I cried. "Have you doubled your prices?"

"Same rate as always, Lord Hades," said Charon. "Two passengers, two gold coins."

"Two passengers?" I said. "Use your eyes, ferryman! It's only me!"

Charon nodded toward something behind me.

I whirled around.

There, hanging on to the back of my chariot, was Persephone.

"Surprise!" she said.

Chapter II

PHONE HOME, PERSEPHONE!

Persephone jumped off the back of my chariot. "What a bumpy ride!"

I was too stunned to say a word. I could only stare at her in disbelief.

"So, this is the Underworld." Persephone peered through the big bronze gates. The inscription above them read:

**WELCOME TO THE UNDERWORLD!
MORTALS EVERYWHERE ARE DYING TO GET IN**

"The place has a nice moonlight glow," she added.

"Get into the chariot, Persephone," I said sternly. "Charon? Take us across the Styx. I have to take a certain sneaky goddess back up to earth."

"Oh, not yet, Hades," Persephone said. "Before I go, can't I have a little tour of your kingdom?"

I folded my arms across my chest. "Not a chance."

Just then I heard wild, joyous barking. My three-headed guard dog, Cerberus, came barreling down the riverbank to greet me.

"Hey, Cerbie!" I said, bending down to receive him as he leaped into my arms. "That's my good boy, boy, boy." He gave my face the old triple-licking as I patted each of his heads in turn.

Cerberus was enjoying himself, wagging his stump of a tail like crazy. Suddenly he froze. He'd spotted Persephone. Deep, hostile rumblings started up from all three of his throats.

Persephone backed up. "Is he growling at *me*?"

"Take it easy, Cerbie," I said, scratching him behind one set of ears. "You don't have to frighten her away, boy. No, because I'm about to take her home."

Hearing this, Cerberus wagged his tail. But he kept on growling.

The last god my dog had growled at was Zeus. But Zeus had tried to zap him with a thunderbolt. Persephone hadn't done anything. Why was Cerberus acting so hostile?

Persephone slowly extended a hand. "Nice doggy?"

Cerberus bared his teeth. I kept soothing him. I didn't want him to snap at her. The last thing I needed was a lawsuit on my hands.

"Hop into the chariot, Persephone," I said again. "I'm taking you home."

"Oh, Hades!" said Persephone. "I've come all this way. Just let me see what the Underworld is like. Please? Besides, it's late. You don't want to drive me all the way up to earth at this hour."

Persephone was right. I was beat—too beat to make the trip again. And so were my steeds. Maybe I'd ask one of the Furies—my immortal avengers— to look after Persephone for one night, and then I could take her home tomorrow.

"All right," I agreed. "You can stay the night. *One* night, and that's it."

Persephone's face lit up. "Thanks, Hades!"

I had a feeling that tomorrow she'd try to talk me into staying another night, and then another. But I was a busy god. I had a kingdom to rule. I couldn't be taking random goddesses on endless tours of the Underworld!

"I'll take you home first thing tomorrow," I went on. "But now you'd better phone home and let your mom know—" I'd started to say "where you are," but I stopped myself in time. I didn't want anyone knowing I'd let a goddess into my kingdom. It could give other gods and goddesses ideas about coming down to see the sights. What a nightmare! My privacy would be shot. I had to be careful. "Let your mom know you're okay," I finished up.

"I will," said Persephone. She jumped into the front seat of my chariot. "Just as soon as you give me the deluxe Underworld tour."

I sat back down in the driver's seat. "I usually make the rounds of my kingdom about this time anyway," I said.

Cerberus leaped into the chariot. He wedged

himself into the space between me and Persephone on the front seat.

"Giddy-up, Harley! Giddy-up, Davidson!" I called.

As we rode through the Underworld Gate, a plan formed itself in my mind. I'd show Persephone the darkest, scariest parts of my kingdom. By tomorrow morning, I wouldn't have to argue with her about going back to earth. She'd be good and ready to go!

I began by driving Persephone through a thick grove of black poplar trees. It was very dark. But Persephone didn't seem to be afraid of the dark. In fact, she didn't seem to notice. She just kept chattering away.

"Don't you think a young goddess should get to have a little fun once in a while?" Persephone said.

"I guess," I answered.

"Well, my mom is not into fun," Persephone said. "She's always on my case to till the soil, water the plants, pull the weeds, harvest the corn, or do some other backbreaking chore. She never lets up! So I decided to take off for a while. When I waved you down, I was hoping to get a ride into Athens. I have some goddess girlfriends who have an apartment—Hey, what's that over there?" she asked, peering through the trees. "Are those cabins?"

"That's Motel Styx," I told her. "It's the temporary quarters for the new ghosts. They stay there until they've been judged."

Dozens of ghosts were lined up outside Motel Styx, waiting to check in. When they saw us drive by, they began moaning and howling horribly. I glanced at Persephone, thinking she'd be shivering in fright. But instead, she was waving at the ghosts, as if she were some sort of Underworld homecoming queen!

Obviously, Persephone wasn't afraid of ghosts.

But I wasn't worried. There were scarier things up ahead. I turned the horses onto a road that curved down a steep hill.

"Over there?" I said, pointing. "That's the Underworld Jail. It's filled with dozens of enormous Titan warriors who have been locked up ever since they lost the big war for Mount Olympus. Every one of them is seething with red-hot anger."

"Cool," said Persephone. "Can we visit the jail? I've never seen a Titan up close and personal."

"Maybe later." I sighed and kept going down the hill. As we went, Cerberus occasionally turned to Persephone and growled.

"Cerbie!" I said. "Cease!"

After a while, he gave me a triple dirty look that said clearly I didn't appreciate what a fine dog he was, or I'd boot Persephone out of the chariot. Then he stacked his heads on his paws and went to sleep. Even the constant ringing from Persephone's purse didn't wake him.

"I'm not picking up," Persephone said as her phone rang and rang. "Mom can't exactly come looking for me down here. But I'll phone home later, I promise."

I nodded, thinking that what I was about to show Persephone might just frighten her enough to phone home right away. We were heading for Tartarus, a deep fiery pit, and the most frightening place in my kingdom. In any kingdom, for that matter. I was absolutely positive that Tartarus would scare the girdle off Persephone.

"You might not like Tartarus," I warned her. "It's a terrible place, where bubbling hot tar and rivers of flaming lava torment the ghosts of the wicked."

"Wow," said Persephone. "I can't wait to see it."

"Maybe some other time," I muttered, and I turned the horses back toward the main road. Tartarus was hot as blazes. I didn't feel like getting covered in *drosis* (old Greek-speak for "god sweat") if Persephone was going to react to it as an attraction in some sort of Underworld theme park.

Was there nothing in my kingdom I could show this goddess to make her want to run screaming home and never come back? I glanced at Persephone. She was looking around with great curiosity. She was a most determined goddess. I had to say that for her. And she didn't frighten easily. There was more to her than sweetness and flowers.

I spurred the horses on. They turned and trotted down a road lined with pomegranate trees. I pointed them out to Persephone. "They're the only trees that bear fruit in this part of the Underworld," I told her. "Ever had a pomegranate?"

Persephone shook her head.

"You should try one," I said. "They're delicious!"

On we went toward the Underworld Traffic Circle. In the middle of it stood the Underworld Courthouse. The Cyclopes had built it, and it was one of the jewels of my kingdom. I reined in the horses so Persephone could take a good look.

"That's where the ghosts are judged," I told her. "They get sent to live in different parts of my kingdom depending on how good or how bad they were while they were alive."

"Don't you feel awful sending ghosts to that red-hot punishment place, Tartarus?" Persephone asked.

"I don't do the judging myself," I told her. "King di Minos does that."

"Hold it," said Persephone. "I thought you were king down here."

"I *am*," I said. "Di Minos was once King of Crete. He still insists on wearing his crown and being called by his title. Zeus is his dad. But his mother was a mortal from Italy, so di Minos was born a mortal, too. When he died, Zeus couldn't stand the thought of one of his children becoming a ghost, so he made di Minos immortal and set him up down here as a judge."

Zeus was always marrying mortals, and it was always a problem when his offspring turned out to be mortal, too. Most immortals knew better and stuck to marrying their own kind.

I could have gone on and on about di Minos. He drove me crazy. I suspected that he was Zeus's spy, and that he told him everything that went on in my kingdom. I'd have to do something about him one of these days.

I whistled to my steeds and steered the chariot from the courthouse into a stretch of colorless turf that extended as far as the eye could see. "The gray plants with the prickly leaves are asphodel," I said. "It's our main crop down here, the only thing that grows in most of the Underworld."

"Ugly stuff," said Persephone. "Stop for a second, Hades. I want to try something."

I pulled on the reins, and Persephone jumped out of the chariot. She ran a short distance. Wherever her feet touched the ground, the asphodel instantly changed from dusty gray to green, and pink blossoms burst open.

"That's amazing," I said. "How did you do that?"

"It's a goddess-of-spring thing," Persephone said, stepping back into the chariot. "I guess you could say it's my talent. I just wanted to see if I could do it in the Underworld."

As we started off again, we saw a group of ghosts wandering around in circles through the asphodel. They were all chanting something under their breaths. "I before E except after C. I before E except after C . . ."

"They're some of the not-so-bad-but-not-so-good ghosts," I told her. "That's who lives in the Asphodel Fields. Their punishment is memorizing an endless list of really hard spelling words."

"Poor ghosts," said Persephone. "No wonder they look so dreary."

I sped up my horses, and at last we came out of the Asphodel Fields. As we did, Persephone said, "Hey, stop! What's that, over there? A *mall*?"

I groaned. I hadn't meant to bring Persephone here. The Underworld Mall was the only part of my kingdom I wasn't proud of. I'd lost the land the mall stood on to di Minos in a poker game. I knew he was cheating, but I couldn't catch him at it. He'd learned to cheat from the expert—Zeus!

"Drive closer, Hades," Persephone said. "Let me see the shops."

"Don't get too excited," I warned her. "After all, the dead in this part of the Underworld *are* being punished."

I drove Persephone toward di Minos Pizza Parlor. Its sign proclaimed: OUR PIZZA IS TO DIE FOR! Di Minos himself suddenly appeared in the doorway. After a day of judging, he always rushed to di Minos Pizza and took over in the kitchen, but he never traded his crown for a chef's hat. Di Minos was a cheat and a spy and a pain in the neck, but I had to admit he was an Underworld-class cook. His pizza was delicious.

I didn't want di Minos to see Persephone, or I'd have to explain who she was and what she was doing down here. I gave my horses a tap, and they put on some speed.

We drove past the rest of the mall shops: di Minos

Decaf Coffee Shop, di Minos Bad-Hair-Day Salon, di Minos One-Size-Fits-All Robe and Tunic Shoppe, and di Minos Movie Palace. A marquee above it announced: NOW SHOWING—SCREAM.

"I see what you mean about the shops," said Persephone. "But at least there's a movie theater."

"That's the only movie it shows," I told her. "Ever."

"What about the ghosts of the good?" she asked. "Where do they live?"

"In Elysium," I said, clicking to my steeds. "I'll show you."

We galloped north through a grove of white cyprus trees. We came close to my palace, Villa Pluto, then we veered east and crossed the bridge over the Pool of Memory. The sky began to brighten. By the time we reached Elysium, the sky overhead was blue.

Persephone gasped as she looked out at the vast orchard, and at the ghosts picnicking in the shade of the apple trees. "This is gorgeous!" she exclaimed.

I nodded. "It pays to be good."

I pointed to the many ghosts heading for a big open-air amphitheater. "They're going to the eternal rock concert, *Rock On!* There's a great band every night."

"Really?" Persephone's eyes lit up. "Who's playing tonight?"

"Shades of Purple," I said.

Persephone squealed. "I LOVE that group! But wait a minute. Those guys are . . ."

"Dead?" I said. "Right. We get all the best bands down here . . . eventually."

"Can I go to the concert, Hades?" Persephone asked. "Please? I mean, Shades of Purple really is my all-time favorite group!"

"All right," I said. I have to admit, I was having fun showing off the cool parts of my kingdom to Persephone. I don't get many live ones down here in the Underworld, and I sort of forgot that the whole point was to make her want to go home.

I checked my watch. "I'll come back and pick you up at XI o'clock."

"Thanks, Hades!" said Persephone. "Keep the picnic basket for me, will you? And my purse?" She jumped out of my chariot and ran toward Elysium. Buttercups sprang up in her footsteps.

Only then did it hit me.

Persephone had forgotten to phone home!

"Persephone!" I yelled "Come back! You forgot to call your mom!"

But she kept on running.

Chapter III

VOICE-MAIL MOM

"Well, Cerbie," I said, after Persephone had disappeared from sight. "Let's go see what's doing at the palace."

Cerberus gave me a little nudge with one of his heads, and I knew we were friends again.

"Home, steeds!" I called. Harley and Davidson took off running. In a short time, I pulled up in front of Villa Pluto. My first clue that something was wrong was the dozens of little white tents pitched all over the palace grounds. "Hypnos!" I called to my first lieutenant. "Hypnos? Where are you?"

Hypnos is the god of sleep, and he lives up to his

name. Most days, I could count on finding him out by the pool, snoozing in the hammock. But that day, he came rushing down the walk to meet me.

"Oh, King Hades! I'm so glad you're here!" he cried. "So many new ghosts have arrived. We don't have room for them all! We are overbooked, overextended, overwhelmed!"

"Take it easy, Hypnos," I said.

He closed his eyes and took a deep breath. And then another breath. And another. I realized he was snoring.

"Hypnos!" I shouted. "Not *that* easy."

"Huh?" He woke with a start. "Oh, King Hades! I'm so glad you're here!"

"You mentioned that," I said. "Now tell me what happened."

"There was a big battle up on earth," Hypnos said. "Many mortals were slain, and Hermes is bringing them down here by the busload. Motel Styx is a disaster. There are ten times more ghosts in every room than the fire code allows. The ghosts are howling their heads off—well, the ones who still have their heads, anyway."

I sighed. Ghosts are so demanding! There isn't much to them, but boy, can they put up a fuss. I spent the next several hours managing the crisis. It was almost XI o'clock by the time I finished. My stomach was growling. I hadn't eaten a thing since I'd grabbed a hot dog at the wrestling match, and I was hungry. But before I could eat, I had to pick up Persephone.

I jumped back into my chariot and galloped over to Elysium.

"Yoo-hoo! Hades!" Persephone ran toward me when she spotted the chariot. "That was the best concert!" she exclaimed. "Fantastic!" She hopped in, bringing the scent of roses with her.

Cerberus sneezed and hunkered down, claiming his spot on the seat between us. He growled softly. Persephone wisely ignored him. "Shades of Purple sang all their classic songs," she told me as we headed for my palace. "The dead mortals knew all the words, so we sang along. I've never had so much fun."

"Glad you liked it," I said. "Listen, your phone's been ringing nonstop. How about phoning home now? Your mom might be worried."

"Might be?" said Persephone. "Ha! She's *always* worried." She took out her purse phone and checked her voice mail. "Look! I have seventy-three messages, and they're all from my mother! What does that tell you? She is so out of control! I can't deal with her right now, Hades. I just can't! But I'll give her a call first thing tomorrow. Honest."

"Okay," I said. "Then you can say you're on your way home."

Persephone's face fell when she heard that. We drove the rest of the way to Villa Pluto in silence. I stopped at the entrance.

"What an awesome palace!" Persephone said. "It's huge! Do you have a throne room? How about a ballroom?" She didn't wait for me to answer, but jumped out of the chariot and ran up the steps. She pushed open the big front door.

I turned the chariot over to a stable-boy ghost and followed Persephone into the marble entryway. "I'm going to order us a pizza." I picked up the nearest phone and punched in the number I knew so well.

"Di Minos Pizza!" a cheery voice answered.

"We deliver in under XXX minutes, or your pie is free!"

I didn't like giving di Minos my business, but what could I do? I was hooked on his pizza. I ordered two extra-large ambrosia-and-sausage pies, and a VI-pack of Necta-Colas.

"Come on down to the den," I said to Persephone. "You can meet my houseguests."

"You have company?" Persephone asked.

"They aren't exactly company," I said. "They live here because they more or less work for me." I led the way down a long hallway and opened the door to the den. I nodded toward an old man conked out in a rocker. "That's Thanatos. He's the actual god of death," I told Persephone. "The one dozing over there under the little blanket? That's his brother, Hypnos, god of sleep."

"Wow, what a fun pair," said Persephone.

A voice came from the couch on the far side of the den: "Aren't you going to introduce me, Hades?"

I turned around. "Tisi!" I exclaimed. "What are you doing home at this hour? Why aren't you up on earth, hounding the wicked and settling scores?"

"I took a night off," Tisi said. She yawned and put her magazine, *Underworld Bizarre*, down on the coffee table. She looked relaxed with her great black wings folded against her back. The dozens of snakes that sprouted from her head were snoozing. Evidently they were taking the night off, too.

"Tisi, this is Persephone, goddess of spring," I said. "Don't ask how she got here. She's leaving first thing tomorrow. Persephone? Meet Tisi, one of the Furies."

Tisi winked a bright red eye and smiled, showing gleaming white fangs. "Hey, Persephone," she said.

Persephone's picnic basket slid from her hand. It took her a few seconds to find her voice. I understood. If you've never seen a Fury before, it's sort of a shock.

Tisi and her sisters, Meg and Alec, had been in the universe for a long time before we gods showed up. When I became King of the Underworld, I built the Furies their own private wing in my palace. I considered the three of them my closest friends. Still, I was always careful not to offend them. The Furies have quick tempers, and when they get angry? Look out! They carry little whips called scourges, made of many leather strips. Each strip ends in a sharp brass tip. Tisi has a special scourge tipped with live scorpions.

"Tisi, hi," Persephone managed at last. Then she dashed across the room and sat down across from her. "Oh, wow, I love your hair. I mean, snakes. And that is such a cool leather minirobe. Did you get it at the mall down here at that Robe and Tunic Shoppe? Because I wouldn't mind having one just like it. But maybe not in black. I'm goddess of spring, so I wear pastels. You know, peach, baby blue, yellow, mint green. . . ."

I smiled. Obviously, Persephone had never met anyone as cool as a Fury. She yakked away about Tisi's great look. And Tisi? I could tell she was enjoying it. Even a Fury likes to be admired now and then.

I only hoped that Persephone wouldn't start complaining about her mother, because things could have gotten very ugly, very fast. The main job of a Fury is to punish ungrateful children who have insulted their mothers. But luckily, Persephone just seemed to want shopping tips, so Tisi kept her claws retracted, and everything was friendly.

I wasn't interested in the whole hair-and-fashion chat, so I made my way over to my La-Z-God recliner. I sat down, flipped up the footrest, and clicked on my big-screen TV. The picture came on. An announcer's voice boomed out, "And now, back to *The Zeus Show!*"

"Tisi?" I called. "Where's the remote?"

Tisi shrugged. "Haven't seen it."

A close-up of Zeus flashed onto the screen. That's the major drawback of having a big-screen TV—Zeus's face is enormous!

Had Hypnos dropped the remote when he dozed off? I jumped up and hurried over to where he was sleeping. I dug under his chair cushions. No remote.

I always used the remote, but I thought there must be a channel changer on the set itself. I ran over to the TV. I searched for an OFF button, but I couldn't find one. Ohhh, who'd tuned into the Zeus Channel, anyway? It was all Zeus, all the time. When it wasn't live, it showed endless reruns. I couldn't imagine why anyone in their right mind wanted to watch Zeus for two seconds, let alone XXIV/VII.

"Are you *sure* the remote isn't over by you?" I asked Tisi.

Tisi shot me an awful red-eyed glare. "Quite sure."

She and Persephone were now deep into a discussion of sandals, and they weren't paying the least bit of attention to me or the TV.

The camera pulled back, and I saw that Zeus was getting a royal rubdown from the Mount Olympus Massage Nymph. Demeter, goddess of agriculture, was standing beside him, ranting.

"She's still missing!" Demeter wailed. "She went out to pick flowers, and that's the last I saw of her! You must find her, Zeus! Find her!"

Demeter hadn't changed a bit since I had last seen her, a few hundred years back. What a drama goddess!

"She'll come home," Zeus said. "Now, uh, go see if my new tree is bearing olives yet, will you, Demeter? I have a sudden craving."

Oooh, Zeus is such a louse. Where was that remote? I got down on my hands and knees and peered under my La-Z-God. Nothing. I crawled over to the couch.

I was still crawling when I heard Demeter howl, "No olives shall ripen! No figs shall fatten! No tomatoes shall redden! No crops of any kind shall grow! Hot winds shall scorch the earth until Persephone comes home!"

Persephone?

I jumped up, banging my head on the coffee table. "Ow!" I rubbed the sore spot. "Persephone?" I said, staring at her.

"Hades?" she said. "What is wrong with you?"

"Your mother is *Demeter*?" I said.

Persephone nodded, and went back to her conversation with Tisi.

Weak in the knees, I plopped down on the nearest chair. Now all Persephone's complaints about having to weed and harvest crops made sense! My sister Demeter, the scariest Olympian of them all, was her mother!

Even when she was a little girl goddess growing

up in Dad's belly, Demeter had been a weirdo. All she could talk about was planting a garden. Then she'd become attached to that stone Mom had fooled Dad into swallowing. Now, I guessed, she was equally obsessed with her daughter. No wonder she kept calling! And if she knew Persephone was in the Underworld, she'd come raging down here to get her. Nothing would stop her.

"Get a life, Demeter," Zeus said. Then to the Massage Nymph, he added, "A little higher on the right shoulder. Ah! That's the spot."

"I shall go to Crete!" Demeter cried. "There, at my shrine, I shall weep and rend my garments until Persephone is found!"

I whisked the blanket off Hypnos and threw it over the TV. Through gritted teeth, I said, "Phone home, Persephone! Tell your mother that you're on your way home *right now*!"

Just then, the palace doorbell rang. A voice called out, "Di Minos!" And the scent of warm pizza wafted into the den as one of my staff let the delivery ghost in.

"Can we eat first, Hades?" said Persephone.

"All right." I was too hungry to argue. "But the second we've finished, I'm taking you home."

Two of my serving ghosts brought in the pizza. Tisi didn't bother with a plate. She extended a single claw, speared a slice, and devoured it in a single elegant gulp. I put a slice on a plate and offered it to Persephone. She took one look at it and wrinkled up her nose.

"Try it," I told her. "Di Minos is a jerk, but he's a whiz with pizza."

Persephone shook her head. "Too greasy," she said. "I'll find something in my basket." She took the plate over to her picnic basket and filled it with what looked like stuffed grape leaves. I shrugged and dug into my pizza.

When we'd finished eating, I turned to Persephone. "A deal's a deal," I said. "Let's get you home."

"Deal?" said Persephone. "I never agreed to any deal, Hades. You saw how my mother is. Please! Let me stay! Just for a few days."

"If Demeter finds out where you are—" I began.

"But she won't!" said Persephone. "How can she? Besides, you need help down here, Hades.

Those Asphodel Fields are so depressing. You saw how I made the asphodel bloom. I could turn those fields into a garden! For a goddess, I'm a very hard worker. I could do flower arrangements for Motel Styx. Or—or I could work with Tisi." She turned to the Fury. "What is it you do, exactly?"

"I'm an avenger," Tisi said. "I hear the complaints of mortals—mostly mothers—who have been wronged by their children. Then my sisters and I punish the offenders."

"I could help with that!" Persephone said. "I'm really into justice."

Tisi only shrugged.

Persephone's words gave me an idea. If I tried to take her back to earth, she'd be protesting the whole way. And then I'd have to deal with Demeter. But what if I got the Furies to take her? Of course, they couldn't exactly tell her they were taking her home. But they could fly her up to Crete and—surprise! Mother-and-daughter reunion. I smiled. It was a perfect plan!

"Oh, all right, Persephone," I said. "I'm not going to argue with you."

"Smart move," said the goddess of spring with a giggle.

"But I have a full schedule tomorrow," I went on. "Hundreds of ghosts to deal with. I won't have a spare minute to spend with you." I turned to Tisi. "How about taking Persephone avenging with you tomorrow?"

Persephone gasped. "Would you, Tisi? That would be so amazing!"

"Hmmm," Tisi said, looking thoughtful. "I don't think we have anything too gruesome lined up for tomorrow. All right, Persephone can come."

"Oh, Tisi! Thank you!" exclaimed Persephone. "Thank you, Hades!"

Tisi stood up and stretched. "Well, I need my beauty rest," she said.

"Me, too," said Persephone. "Totally."

"The Furies wing is through that door," I told Persephone, nodding toward it. "Go have a look around. I need a private word with Tisi. She'll be there in a minute to show you which bedroom you can have."

Persephone smiled. "Good night, Hades. And

thanks for the greatest day of my life!" Then she scampered through the doorway. I felt sort of bad, thinking how I was about to trick her. She had such a trusting smile. But it seemed the only way to get her back to her mother.

I turned to Tisi. "You must have figured out by now that Persephone has run away from home," I said. "From her mother."

Tisi's red eyes widened in surprise. I guessed she really hadn't been paying attention to *The Zeus Show*. On hearing this, Tisi's snakes woke up and started swaying.

"Her mother is Demeter," I went on, "goddess of agriculture. She's desperate to have her daughter back. She's in Crete right now, sobbing and carrying on. You know how upset mothers can get when they're worried about their children."

The snakes were really riled up now, squirming and hissing.

"We avenge the wrongs of mortals, Hades," Tisi said. "Not goddesses."

"Okay, Persephone's a goddess," I told Tisi. "But her mom's still a mom. And if you take Persephone home to her, I guarantee Demeter will be the happiest mother in the universe. Of course you'll have to . . . surprise Persephone," I added. "Take her on one or two avenging missions. Then fly her over to Crete. You'd be doing a great good deed."

Tisi thought for a moment. Then she said. "It sounds like the right thing to do, Hades. I'm sure Meg and Alec will agree."

I smiled. "Sleep well, my avenger."

"I always do," Tisi said. Then she drew closer to me. Her eyes sparkling like rubies, she whispered, "Hades, Persephone has such a crush on you!"

Then she, too, disappeared into the Furies wing.

I stood frozen to the spot.

Never in my life had I heard such horrible, terrible words.

Chapter IV

LONG DISTANCE

The next morning, I hummed to myself as I hitched Harley and Davidson to my big VI-seater chariot. I jumped in. Cerberus hopped in beside me. The Furies and Persephone climbed into the backseat, and off we galloped for the River Styx. When we reached the Underworld Gate, I reined in my steeds. "Here we are, ladies."

"We could have flown," said Tisi.

"But thanks for the ride, Hades!" said Meg sweetly. As always, she wore her serpents in a perky ponytail.

"Flying would have been *much* faster," grumbled

Alec. Her snakes are short and stubby, and stick straight up all over her head.

"I know, I know," I said. "But I wanted to say good-bye to Persephone. Going off on one's first avenging trip is a big deal." I turned to the goddess of spring. "Well, bye!"

Cerberus had three brains, and he'd figured out that Persephone was leaving. He ran in happy circles around her as she got out of the chariot.

"I'm so excited, Hades," Persephone said. "I'll see you late tonight and tell you all about it!"

"Ready?" Tisi asked.

"Ready!" Persephone said.

Meg and Alec bent down. They clasped each other's forearms, making a seat for Persephone. She sat down.

Thwap! Tisi unfurled her great black wings. With a single flap, they lifted her up. Meg and Alec took off next, carrying Persephone. I watched until all I could see of them were dark specks against the Underworld sky.

"Yessss!" I said to myself. "One goddess of the spring, gone for good!"

Cerbie and I got back into my chariot. I whistled to my steeds, and we headed over to Motel Styx. We were cruising around the kingdom as usual, just my dog and me. I could tell Cerberus was happy to have things back to normal. I was, too.

It was another crazy day in the Underworld. Charon brought over the rest of the ghosts from the big battle, and Motel Styx filled up again. I made sure things were running as smoothly as possible there, then headed over to the courthouse.

On my way, I glanced over at the Asphodel Fields. I saw the place where Persephone's footsteps had made the asphodel bloom. The little pink flowers were starting to droop now, but their smell hung in the air. That sweet scent reminded me of Persephone. It had been kind of fun having her around, showing her my kingdom, and answering all of her questions. She seemed happy in the Underworld. If she ever came back, I thought—but I quickly stopped myself. What was wrong with me, anyway? I'd just gotten rid of that pesky goddess. The last thing I wanted was to have her back again!

It was nightfall by the time I found a place for all

the new ghosts to sleep. I left Hypnos in charge of actually getting them to sleep, and I headed back to Villa Pluto. It had been a long, hard day. I was looking forward to putting my feet up in front of the TV and enjoying a nice cold Necta-Cola.

When I got back to the palace, that's just what I did. I relaxed into my La-Z-God, and clicked on the tube. I'd finally found the remote on the coffee table, under my Helmet of Darkness. I surfed around for a while, then stopped on the Wrestling Channel. What luck! A really great match was on. "Eagle Eye" Cyclops was taking on "Hugs" Python. As always, I started rooting for the Cyclops.

"Keep your eye on him, Cyclops!" I yelled at the set. "Come on! You can take the snake!"

The snake was down! The referee started counting: "I! II! III! IV! V!—"

Just then I got the feeling that I was being watched. I glanced quickly over my shoulder. The Furies were home. I flashed on the fact that they were back early. But the wrestling match was in its final seconds, so I didn't pay much attention. I barely managed a "Hey, ladies."

"VI!" called the ref. "VII! VIII!"

Behind me, I felt the Furies' smoldering presence. It wasn't easy, but I tore my eyes from the screen and looked at them. They stood together, the three of them, glaring angrily down at me.

An unhappy Fury is a terrible thing.

Three unhappy Furies?

That's an emergency.

I quickly clicked off the TV. "My own avengers!" I said, hopping up out of my chair. "Is something wrong?"

"We carried out your plan, Hades," said Tisi. Her scorpion-tipped whip was still sticking out of her pocket. "We returned Persephone to her mother."

"Her mother was so very happy," said Meg.

"But Persephone was *not*," said Alec.

"Well, we expected that, didn't we? Sit," I added, patting the couch. "Start at the beginning. Tell me everything. Whatever's wrong, I'll fix it."

"Oh, thank you, Hades," said Meg with a sweet, fang-filled smile.

The Furies sat down on the couch. I took a seat facing them.

"We flew up to earth on our mission of vengeance," Tisi began. "Our first appointment was with a young man in Athens. He had forgotten Mother's Day."

Meg sighed. "He hadn't even sent a card."

"We flew around him, shrieking and rattling our scourges," said Alec. "He fell to his knees and begged for mercy."

"It was a first offense, so we let him off with only a warning," said Tisi.

"Good judgment call," I told them.

"Our next appointment was with a young maiden in Athens," Tisi said. "She had served her mother breakfast in bed."

"It was a lovely thing to do," Meg said. "But when the mother came into the kitchen, she found the sink piled high with dirty dishes."

"Egg stuck on the skillet," said Alec. *"Yecch!"*

"Oh, dear," I said.

"We took the first deed into account," said Tisi. "We merely hounded the girl from house to house in her neighborhood, and made her wash everyone's dishes."

"A fitting punishment," I said.

"Then we flew to Crete," said Tisi. "Persephone believed we were going to avenge another wrong."

"We told her to close her eyes," said Meg. "We said we had a surprise for her."

"We spotted Demeter sitting on a big stone, weeping," said Alec. "Even gods and goddesses cower in fear when they see us flying toward them. But Demeter never flinched."

"We set her daughter down before her," Tisi said. "Demeter sprang up and wrapped her arms around Persephone."

"She hugged her daughter for the longest time," said Meg.

"Like *forever!*" said Alec.

"Demeter finally let go," said Tisi. "And Persephone turned toward us."

"She gave us an awful look," said Meg.

"A look that said, 'How could you betray me like this?'" Alec added.

"And for the very first time in our very long lives," said Tisi, "we three Furies were stricken with alarming pangs of conscience."

"Conscience?" I said. Who knew Furies even had consciences?

"We are avengers," said Tisi. "We right wrongs. We settle scores. We inflict terrible punishments on evildoers. But tricking Persephone was the first time we had ever done wrong ourselves."

"It was unforgivable," said Meg.

"It was the *worst*," said Alec.

I didn't know what to say. I only hoped they'd get over it—and quickly.

"We could not undo our deed," Tisi went on. "But we three went to Persephone."

"We said we were sorry," said Meg.

"*Very* sorry," said Alec.

"We begged Persephone to think of some way for us to make up for what we'd done," said Tisi. "She thought for a while. At last, she said there *was* something we could do."

I felt a knot forming in the pit of my stomach. "And what was that, my most fearful avengers?"

"We are to ask you to come up to earth to have a picnic with Persephone," said Meg.

"A picnic?" The knot in my stomach tightened.

"She says to come to the field outside Athens where you met her yesterday," said Tisi. "She'll bring the food and drinks."

"All you have to do is show up," said Alec.

"And be nice to her, Hades," added Meg. "She likes you!"

My stomach was now one large and complicated knot.

"And when is this event to take place, my lovely vindicators?" I asked.

In one voice, the Furies answered: "Tomorrow."

Chapter V

LOVE CONNECTION

I wasn't whistling the next morning as I hitched Harley and Davidson to my chariot.

"Hop in, Cerbie," I said. "You can come with me today, boy."

The dog wagged his stumpy tail and leaped into the chariot. I rarely took Cerberus up to earth, but today I wanted some protection. I had a bad feeling about this picnic. A very bad feeling. I tossed my Helmet of Darkness into the backseat, too. If Demeter showed up, I'd need all the help I could get.

I took my time traveling to earth. But when I

finally rode up the last rocky passage and drove my horses out of my secret cave, I could tell right away that Demeter hadn't been joking about her scorched-earth policy. As far as I could see, the grass was brown. Every bush and tree had dropped its leaves.

I rode through the desolate landscape until I came to the place where Persephone had flagged me down two days before. I spotted her sitting in a field of dried-up wildflowers. Today she had on a peach-colored robe with a matching headband and girdle. An enormous picnic basket sat beside her. Spread out on the ground in front of her was a big blue-and-white checkered cloth with platters of food on it. I didn't see Demeter. That was a good thing.

Persephone waved and called, "Hi, Hades!"

I waved back as I rode over to her. When I got out of my chariot, I saw that clover, violets, and sweet buttercups had popped up everywhere Persephone had stepped as she set out the picnic. I unhitched my horses to let them graze.

"Come on, Cerbie," I said. "Picnic time."

"Oh, Hades, can't the dog stay in the chariot?" said Persephone.

"Where I go, my dog goes," I said firmly. "But he'll be good. Won't you boy, boy, boy?"

Cerberus wagged his tail and followed me eagerly to the picnic cloth.

I sat down across from Persephone. Cerberus sat beside me. He leaned forward and started sniffing at the picnic platters with all three noses.

"Stop that!" cried Persephone. "Bad dog!"

Cerberus froze. He gazed up at Persephone with a terrible wounded look in all six eyes. Then he turned and slunk away, his stubby tail between his legs.

I jumped up and ran after my dog. "Cerbie! Wait, boy!" I caught up with him, knelt down, and patted him. "Persephone didn't mean it. No, she didn't. You're a *good* dog! That's right." I looked over my shoulder at Persephone. "No one's ever called him a b-a-d d-o-g before," I said. "Maybe if you apologized?"

"To a dog?" said Persephone. "I don't think so."

I soothed Cerberus a bit more. Then I scooped

him up and carried him back to the picnic. I put him down beside the cloth. He turned around a couple of times and finally lay down, facing away from Persephone.

"Don't worry, boy," I told him. "I'll share."

While I was seeing to Cerberus, Persephone had filled a plate with a little bit of everything she'd brought.

"I forgive you, Hades," she said, as she handed me the plate.

"For bringing my dog?" I took a bite of ambrosia potato salad. "Mmm."

Persephone shook her head. "I know you talked the Furies into tricking me and taking me back to Mom. I know you were trying to do what you thought was right," she went on, filling my goblet with nectar. "I can understand that."

I nodded and kept eating.

"I invited you on this picnic to show that I have no hard feelings." Persephone dabbed at her mouth with her napkin. "Mom says I have to be home by III o'clock, so I can't stay long. But I wanted to see you. I didn't want us to part on bad terms."

I nodded some more. All I could think to say was, "This potato salad is really good."

"I'm glad you like it, Hades." Persephone smiled. "I got it at Martha's of Olympus. They catered Zeus and Hera's wedding. I was in it, did I tell you that?"

I shook my head as I bit into a pickle. Ambrosia dill. Yum!

"I was a bridesmaid," Persephone went on. "One of fourteen! It was such a beautiful ceremony. Hera's dress was awesome."

While I ate, Persephone told me all about the wedding. "You know, Zeus has been married six times before," Persephone said. "But Hera says this time is lucky seven, and that she and Zeus are going to stay married forever."

"Mmmm," I said, helping myself to the coleslaw.

"And do you know how Zeus proposed?" Persephone was saying.

I shook my head. The slaw was tasty, too.

"Oh, it was so romantic," said Persephone. "Zeus had been after Hera to marry him for three hundred years. But Hera couldn't stand his boasting and his myth-o-mania, so she wouldn't have anything to do him. Then one night, Zeus saw Hera all alone, looking out the window of her palace. He grabbed his Bucket o' Bolts and started throwing T-bolts left and right. He made this gigantic thunderstorm, with pouring rain and lightning and everything. Then Zeus turned himself into a little cuckoo and he flew up to Hera's window. Hera felt sorry for the little bird, fluttering around in the storm, so she opened her window and let it come inside. The bird flew to her, and she hugged it to warm it. Then suddenly, the bird disappeared, and Hera found herself hugging Zeus."

"You call *that* romantic?" I said. "I call it sneaky." You never could trust Zeus to do anything straightforward.

While Persephone yakked away about the wedding, I ate my way through her picnic. I managed to sneak Cerberus plenty of scraps, too, when Persephone wasn't looking. I was just wondering whether it would be rude to ask if there were any more ambrosia potato salad, when I heard a faint *zing!* Then I felt a sudden sharp sting on the back of my neck.

"Ow!" I cried, slapping my neck. Had a bee stung me?

"What's wrong, Hades?" asked Persephone. "Did you swallow a bone?"

Cerberus started circling me, whimpering.

I felt around on my neck. There was a little sticky *ichor* (old Greek-speak for "god blood"). Then I felt something poking into my flesh. Something prickly. A thorn? A bee stinger? I yanked it out. It was a tiny golden arrow. Where had that come from?

A sudden dizziness came over me then, and my eyes rolled up into my head.

"Hades?" Persephone was saying. "Hades? Are you all right?"

Her voice sounded far away.

I blinked and managed to focus again. I looked at Persephone. And that's when it hit me like a ton of ambrosia potato salad. Persephone was the most beautiful, the kindest, loveliest, most adorable goddess I'd ever laid eyes on. It seemed incredible that it had taken me so long to notice!

Cerberus was still nudging me and whimpering. But I felt fine now. More than fine. I wasn't dizzy anymore, but my head swirled with one happy thought. A thought too big and too wonderful to keep inside my head. I had to—*had to*—shout it out to all the world.

I jumped to my feet and ran across the picnic cloth to Persephone, knocking platters and plates and goblets every which way. I grabbed her hands in mine.

"Hades!" Persephone exclaimed. "What's gotten into you?"

"Persephone!" I cried. "I love you!"

Persephone gasped. "Do you really?"

"Yes!" I shouted. "I love you! I love you! I love you!"

Cerberus began running madly around us, barking his heads off. Then he sank his teeth—all three sets of them—into the hem of my robe. He tried to pull me away from Persephone.

"Stop, Cerberus!" I said in my most commanding voice. "Down, boy, boy, boy!"

Cerbie let go of my robe. He let out an awful triple-throated howl.

I ignored him as I fell to my knees before

Persephone. "My darling, Persephone," I began, with the chorus of howls in the background, "Marry me!"

"NoooooooooOOOOOOO!" howled the Cerberus trio.

"Cerbie, quiet!" I ordered. I turned back to Persephone. "Come with me to the Underworld, and rule as my queen!"

"Queen Persephone." Persephone giggled. "That has a nice ring to it. But this is so sudden, Hades. I need time to think."

"Certainly, my darling," I said. "Take all the time you need."

Persephone tapped her lovely fingers on her darling chin a few times. Then she looked up at me and said, "All right, Hades. Let's get married!"

"Oh, joy!" I shouted. I was the happiest god in the universe.

Cerberus howled mournfully.

"Let us go to the Underworld now, my sweet," I said to Persephone. "The sooner we get there, the sooner we can be wed."

Cerberus picked that minute to dash off into the bushes.

"Cerbie! Come back!" I cried.

But he kept running.

I quickly helped Persephone pack up the food. I'd eaten plenty, but there was lots left over. I put the picnic basket on the backseat of the chariot.

"Cerberus, come!" I called again. But he stayed in the bushes, snarling and barking.

"Let's not worry about the dog," said Persephone. "He'll find his way home."

Cerberus's barking reached a frantic pitch. Suddenly a young god burst out of the bushes with Cerberus hot on his heels.

Here was another god I'd never met. He was hardly more than a boy-god, really. He had a bow and a quiver of arrows slung over one shoulder.

"Help me!" the god cried. "Somebody call off this mutt!"

"Cerberus!" I called. "Come!"

At my command, Cerberus gave the god a final snarl and trotted back to me. He whimpered loudly, even as I stroked one of his heads.

Persephone put a hand above her eyes to shade them from the sun.

"Why, I believe that's Aphrodite's son, Cupid," she said. "I wonder what he's doing here."

She waved, and Cupid started jogging over to us. He was a pale young god with yellow curls.

Cupid stopped some distance from us. "That dog is really scary, man," he said.

"He won't hurt you," I said. "He only attacks at my command."

Cerberus bared three sets of teeth at Cupid and gave a low, menacing growl.

"Cerberus!" I said. "Be still!"

"Hi, Cupid," said Persephone. "You can be the first to hear our good news." She gave him a wink. "Hades and I are engaged!"

That wink! It made me want to punch Cupid in the nose.

Persephone must have seen how I felt. She threw her arms around me and said, "Isn't that right, Hades?"

"That's right," I said through clenched teeth.

"Well, we were just taking off for the Underworld," Persephone told Cupid. "Hope you can come to the wedding! Bye!"

"Yeah, okay," said Cupid. "And what about the . . . you know?"

"Later, Cupid!" Persephone called with a wave. She began pulling me toward my chariot.

Cerberus stuck to me like *kolla* (old Greek-speak for "glue") as I rounded up Harley and Davidson and put them in their harnesses again. The whole time, the dog whined and whimpered at me. At last I bent down and stroked him. "What is it, boy?" I said. "What are you trying to tell me?"

Cerberus's eyes darted to Persephone. "Grrrrr!" he growled. He looked over at Cupid, who still stood in the field. "Hmmm," he whined. Then he jumped up and licked my neck right in the tender spot.

"You're a good boy, boy, boy," I said, patting each of his heads. "And now I know what you're trying to tell me."

Cerberus's tail started wagging like crazy.

"You've had me to yourself all these years," I said. "And you're not sure you want to share me with Persephone. That's it, isn't it, boy?"

"Wrrrrrooooooonnnggg!" yowled Cerberus. "Wrrrrrooooooonnnggg! Wrrrrrooooooonnnggg!"

"Come on, pup," I said. "Let's go."

Cerberus charged into the chariot. He sat down in his usual place on the front seat, spreading out and taking up as much space as possible.

Persephone eyed him and thumbed in the direction of the backseat.

Cerberus sat firm.

"Jump in the back, Cerbie," I said. "Come on, pup. That's my boy."

Cerberus gave me a withering look. Then he slowly stood up and made his way into the backseat.

I sat down in the driver's seat, and Persephone sat down beside me.

"Giddy-up, steeds!" I said.

As we started off, Persephone turned around in her seat. She smiled at Cerberus. "Get used to it back there, dog," she said.

Chapter VI

RING!

As we galloped down to the Underworld, my darling Persephone talked on and on about plans for our wedding. How I admired her! We had been engaged only a few moments, yet the event was already fully formed inside her lovely head.

Charon taxied us across the Styx. This time I was glad to pay the extra fare for Persephone, my queen-to-be. Once on the other side of the river, we went straight to Villa Pluto.

"I have an idea, Hades," Persephone said as we pulled up in front. "Let's invite a few friends over tonight for an engagement party."

"A, uh, party, my dear?" I swallowed. I'd never had a party in Villa Pluto. I'd never had a party anywhere, for that matter. But Persephone looked so excited about the idea. How could I say no? "What a wonderful idea, my beloved!"

Persephone gave me a hug. "I'll take care of everything!" she said, and she ran into the palace.

I took my steeds to the stable and handed them over to my ghostly grooms. I was too much in love to deal with the usual demands of ruling the Underworld that afternoon, so I headed over to the Cyclopes Village. I wanted to tell Uncle Shiner the big news myself.

On the way to see my uncle, I stopped by one of my caves. Like all my Underworld caves, its walls were studded with gold, silver, and jewels. I pried what I thought was a large yet tasteful heart-shaped diamond from the wall, then hurried on to the Cyclops blacksmith forge. There I found my uncle hammering a piece of bronze to make a new doorknob for the courthouse.

"Uncle Shiner!" I called over the noise of the bellows.

He raised his safety uni-goggle. "Hades!" he exclaimed when he saw me. He put down his hammer, threw an arm over my shoulder, and we walked outside together.

"I am delighted to see you, nephew," Uncle Shiner said. "Tell me, what is the reason for this unexpected visit?"

"I have news, Uncle Shiner," I said. "I'm getting married!"

Uncle Shiner's eye opened wide. "Well! Congratulations!" he said. "*Mazel tov!* And what is the name of the fortunate goddess who shall become your bride?"

"Persephone," I told him. "Goddess of spring."

"We could use some spring down here," he said, smiling.

As we walked, I told him about Persephone's lovely eyes and how good she smelled and how flowers sprang up in her footsteps. We sat down on a bench beside Lethe, the Pool of Forgetfulness.

"And how long have you been courting Persephone?" Uncle Shiner asked.

"I haven't exactly courted her, Uncle Shiner,"

I said. "I only met her the day before yes-terday."

"Ah," said Uncle Shiner. "So it was love at first sight."

"Not at all," I said. "I mean, I thought she was cute when I first saw her. But then she tricked me into giving her a ride down here, and it really made me mad."

"Tricked you, eh?" Uncle Shiner chuckled.

I nodded. "It wasn't until this afternoon that I fell in love with her. We were having a picnic. It was very sudden."

"Sudden?" Uncle Shiner blinked.

I nodded. "It just hit me. *Bam!* I was in love."

"Huh." Uncle Shiner seemed puzzled. "Well, love is unpredictable."

"Wait until you meet her, Uncle," I said. "She's wonderful."

Then from the pocket of my robe I drew the heart-shaped diamond. I asked Uncle Shiner to make a ring for Persephone, and to bring it to our engagement party that night.

"I am honored that you have asked me," Uncle

Shiner said. "I shall make a beautiful ring to hold this diamond for the future Queen of the Underworld."

That night, I put on my best robe. I felt so proud as I strode into the candlelit ballroom with Cerberus at my heels. The place was packed with Underworld types. I spotted di Minos's crown in the crowd. Who'd invited him? There was Campe, the Underworld Jail Keep. She sat on the big couch, in front of the fireplace, chatting with the Hundred-Handed Ones and the Cyclopes. When Uncle Shiner saw me, he hurried over and handed me the ring. It was a beauty.

The serving ghosts circled with platters of little hot-underdogs on toothpicks and goblets of chilled champagne—Underworld Bubbly, CDLVI B.C. (Before Cronus).

The Furies arrived late. They always liked to make an entrance in their party clothes—red leather minirobes and sandals with real snakes winding around their legs for straps.

When I saw that everyone at the party had a

drink in hand, I went over and stood beside my darling goddess of spring. I clinked my goblet.

"I have an announcement!" I said.

The guests murmured, then grew still.

"Greetings, Underworldians," I said. "I'm glad that all of you could be here tonight to hear my great good news. Persephone"—I gestured toward her with my goblet—"and I are engaged to be married."

Everyone gasped with surprise.

"I hope this will make it official." I slipped the diamond onto Persephone's finger.

When she saw the ring, Persephone squealed so loudly that she nearly deafened me.

Then all my friends started clapping and cheering. The Cyclopes congratulated me and slapped me on the back. The Hundred-Handed Ones did the same, which took quite a while. I'd never seen the Furies so delighted. They buzzed around Persephone, talking shoes and veils and gowns.

Everyone was celebrating. Everyone except Cerberus. But I saw that Uncle Shiner had squatted down next to him and was patting him consolingly. My good Cyclops uncle. What would I do without him?

Persephone flitted excitedly from guest to guest, showing off her ring. At last she came over and gave me a little peck on the cheek.

"I'm so happy, Hades," she said.

"Me, too," I told her.

"I have to tell Mom the good news!" Persephone unzipped her purse and took out her phone.

I had a bad feeling about that call. "Persephone, my pet . . ." I began.

But she had already punched #I on the memory dial.

"Mom?" Persephone said. "Hi!" She listened for a moment. "No, I'm not out of money again," she said. "I have some really great news. Hades and I are getting married!" Persephone listened again. Then she said, "You're immortal, Mom, so it *can't* be over your dead body."

That didn't sound good.

Persephone kept listening and saying things like, "He did not!" and "No! Of course not!" At last she said, "I don't know where you're getting your information, Mom, but it's totally wrong!" She hung up then, and turned to me. She did not look happy.

"Uh-oh," I said.

"Mom says she's going to get Zeus and the rest of the Olympians," Persephone said. "She's going to lead them all down here to rescue me."

"Rescue you?" I was stunned. "That seems a little over the top."

"I know," Persephone agreed. "She seems to think you've kidnapped me."

"Who, *me*?" I said. "A kidnapper?"

Persephone nodded. "Mom thinks I'm being held here against my will."

What was going on? Maybe getting married had been a sudden decision. I could see how it might take Demeter some time to get used to it. But accusing me of kidnapping? She knew me better than that.

The Furies rushed over to Persephone. They swarmed around her, telling her not to worry.

"That's right, my darling," I said, taking

Persephone's hand in mine. "In fact, let's get married now—tonight!"

But Persephone shook her head. "Oh, Hades," she said. "No goddess wants a spur-of-the-moment wedding!"

"No?" It seemed like a perfectly good idea to me.

"No," Persephone said firmly. "I've always dreamed of a big, splashy wedding with all the trimmings. I want it to be every bit as big and splashy as Zeus and Hera's wedding, and I want to invite everyone from Mount Olympus."

The idea of the Underworld filled with Olympian wedding guests filled me with dread. But I was so in love with Persephone that I was willing to endure even that. "Then," I said, "we must have just such a wedding."

"But a big, splashy wedding takes planning," said Persephone. "And Mom and the rest of the Olympians will be here in only nine days. We can't pull off what I have in mind that fast."

Now Tisi stepped forward. "Of course we can," the Fury said. "Nine days from today, Persephone— the moment the Olympians arrive—you and Hades are going to have the biggest, splashiest wedding ever held in the universe!"

Persephone gave a little squeal of happiness. She opened her arms and threw them around the Fury.

"When your mother sees your gown," Tisi went on, "and how we've decorated for the wedding, she'll know you haven't been kidnapped." She smiled, and her fangs gleamed in the candlelight. I had a feeling that planning this wedding was her way of making it up to Persephone for tricking her.

Just then, Uncle Shiner tapped me on the shoulder. "Hades," he said, "might I have a word with you?"

I nodded, and followed him outside onto a ballroom balcony. Cerberus tagged along.

"The ring is a work of art, Uncle Shiner," I told him. "Thank you."

The Cyclops nodded. "Hades," he said, "are you sure you know what you're getting into here?"

In truth, I had been wondering, just the teeniest bit, how my life would change after the wedding. I was used to being on my own. I had my dog for company, and I was set in my bachelor ways. I liked ordering pizza for dinner. And kicking back in front of the TV to eat it while I watched wrestling. Now Persephone would be always at my side. She didn't like pizza. And it was sort of hard to picture her beside me kicked back in a matching La-Z-Goddess, watching wrestling and rooting for the Cyclops. What would married life be like?

"Hades?" Uncle Shiner's voice jolted me out of my thoughts. "What I'm asking is, how well do really you know Persephone?"

"Well enough to know she's the goddess of my dreams," I said.

Cerberus whimpered when he heard this.

"You say it was very sudden," Uncle Shiner went on, "the way you fell in love with Persephone?"

I nodded. What was he getting at?

"Did you by any chance see Cupid anywhere near the spot where this happened?" asked Uncle Shiner.

"Yes!" I said, amazed at Uncle Shiner. Out of all the gods in the cosmos, he had picked the very one we saw! "He was the first god we told of our engagement."

I could tell that Uncle Shiner had more to say to me, but just then Persephone rushed out to the balcony.

"There you are, Hades," she said. "You're missing our engagement party! Come inside. You, too, Shiner. Hypnos is about to make a toast."

But my uncle shook his head. He stayed out on the balcony. And for the first time ever, Cerberus didn't follow me. He stayed on the balcony with Uncle Shiner.

The next morning, I was sitting in the kitchen, drinking my nectar cappuccino and reading the Underworld newspaper, *The Hot Times*, when all three Furies showed up. They weren't big on breakfast, but had come to tell me that they were taking a week off to help prepare for the wedding.

"But what about the wicked?" I asked. "Who will hound them while you're away?"

"Don't worry, Hades," said Meg. "We'll avenge on weekends for a while to make up the time."

Over the next three days, Tisi convinced

everyone to pitch in and help with the wedding. She was determined that when the high and mighty Olympians arrived, they would be dazzled by the wonders of the Underworld.

Persephone asked the Furies to be her bridesmaids. Alec stitched up the bridesmaids' dresses and Meg made a wedding gown for Persephone. The Hundred-Handed Ones sewed on thousands and thousands of tiny pearls in practically no time at all.

Tisi ordered something called a toga-tux for me to wear. "It's the latest thing from Rome," she said. "It'll look great on you, Hades."

King di Minos volunteered to cater the wedding feast. Uncle Thunderer worked in the forge to make an extra-long metal table for the wedding supper. Uncle Lightninger offered to take the wedding pictures. My gardener, Cal, said he'd do up the asphodel, whatever that meant. I drove Persephone over to Elysium so she could personally ask Shades of Purple to play at our wedding reception. They said they'd be delighted.

All the plans seemed to be falling into place. It

made me feel good to think that everyone in the Underworld was looking forward to the wedding and to having Persephone become their Queen.

Well, not everyone. Uncle Shiner didn't volunteer to help with anything. And I'd never seen Cerberus so down. When he walked, his heads drooped so low that his chins nearly scraped the ground.

"Snap out of it, Cerbie," I said when I saw him slouching by one morning. "Come on, dog. I'll throw the discus with you for a while."

As he followed me glumly out of the palace, who should be coming up the walk but Uncle Shiner. Cerberus perked up and wagged his tail when he saw the Cyclops.

"I'd like a word with you about Persephone, Hades," said Uncle Shiner.

I didn't like the tone of his voice. "Can't it wait until after the wedding, Uncle Shiner?"

"It most definitely cannot," said Uncle Shiner.

"Can it wait until after a little game of discus?" I asked. "I promised Cerbie."

Uncle Shiner shook his head.

I sighed. "All right." I sat down on the palace steps. "Out with it, Uncle."

"Hades, my boy—" Uncle Shiner began.

But that's as far as he got, because at that instant, Tisi appeared.

"Hades?" she said. "We have a problem."

Chapter VII

CALL IT OFF?

"Is it Persephone?" I asked, jumping to my feet. "Is she all right?"

"She's fine," said Tisi. "But she needs help. Come on. I'll explain while we drive." She grabbed me by the arm and began pulling me down the front steps of the palace.

To tell the truth, I wasn't all that sorry to have my little talk with Uncle Shiner interrupted. "Come, Cerberus!" I called. "Let's go!"

But Cerberus sat down beside Uncle Shiner. He clearly wasn't into helping Persephone.

"I'll take care of him, Hades," Uncle Shiner offered.

With a wave of thanks, I hurried after Tisi to my chariot. A minute later, we were galloping toward the Underworld Mall.

"Persephone is at the pizza parlor with di Minos now," Tisi said.

"A bit early for pizza, isn't it?" I asked.

"She's not there for the pizza, Hades," Tisi said. "Di Minos has set up a table in the asphodel in the front of his restaurant. His waiters are bringing Persephone samples of the food he wants to serve at the wedding banquet. But Persephone says that the menu is all wrong."

"Uh-oh," I said. I'd had a feeling this might happen. The whole time Persephone had been in the Underworld, she'd refused to eat anything but the food she'd brought down in her picnic basket.

"Di Minos keeps telling her to taste the food," Tisi went on. "His waiters are down on their knees, begging her to try just one teensy bite."

"And will she?" I said.

"Take a guess." Tisi sighed. "She's a lovely goddess, Hades, but as stubborn as a mule."

We reached the mall. Tisi and I hurried around to where the table had been set up in front of di Minos Pizza. Nearby, I saw Cal clipping an asphodel hedge into the shape of a swan. I had to smile. So this was his way of getting the Underworld ready for our wedding!

Persephone was sitting at a long table with many platters spread out on it. Di Minos and his waiters stood before her, coaxing her to eat.

"Try an asphodel-cheese puff!" di Minos ordered. "You'll like it! Come on! One bite won't kill you!"

"I'm immortal," said Persephone. "Nothing will kill me. But that puff stuff looks gross, and I'm not eating it."

Di Minos glanced over and saw me coming. "Hades!" he cried. "For once, I'm glad to see you. Listen to this menu!" He began pointing to various dishes. "For starters we pass around asphodel cheese puffs, asphodel-stuffed olives, and asphodel chips with pomegranate dip. Delicious!" He kissed his fingertips and opened them in the air.

"Then the guests sit down, and we serve them

cream-of-asphodel soup. After that come the grilled asphodel burgers. The finest! Served with mashed asphodel root and sautéed asphodel greens. And for dessert? A seven-layer asphodel strudel! You tell her, Hades. This is a banquet fit for the gods!"

"It sounds good to me, Persephone," I said.

My bride-to-be gave me such a look. "Asphodel, asphodel, asphodel, Hades!" she said. "Asphodel strudel is *not* a wedding cake!"

"Well, asphodel is our major crop down here, beloved," I said.

"Taste the strudel, Persephone," added Tisi. "Really, di Minos is a genius with asphodel."

"What do you say, Persephone?" I asked.

My darling looked at me and then at Tisi, di Minos, and the waiters.

"I . . . I guess all of you who have lived in the Underworld for a long time are used to eating asphodel," she said, her voice unsteady. "And it's true, I haven't tasted it. But to me, it just looks really, really icky. I know it's important to serve Underworld-grown food," she added, with a glance at Tisi. "So I was thinking. . . ." She turned to di Minos. "Maybe you could do something more with the pomegranates?"

Di Minos shrugged. "A little pomegranate sorbet to go with the strudel?"

"That's a start," Persephone said. "Now, let's lose the strudel and—" She stopped midsentence. Her eyes widened and her mouth dropped open.

The rest of us turned to see what she was staring at. There, tramping through the asphodel, came Demeter. Behind her were Zeus, Hera, Poseidon, Hestia, Hermes, Aphrodite, Cupid, Apollo, Artemis, Dionysus, and more—the whole gang from Mount Olympus!

I closed my eyes. I hoped I was having some sort of weird pre-wedding hallucination. But when I opened them again, there they were. My nightmare had come true. My kingdom was being invaded by Olympians!

But how had they gotten down here so quickly? It hadn't been nine days since Persephone had phoned home. It had been four days at most. Then I spotted Hermes, all decked out in a shiny new winged helmet and sandals. There was my answer.

Obviously Demeter and Zeus had bribed him to reveal my shortcut through the cave. What a traitor!

Demeter's eyes shone with a crazed gleam as she led her army of Olympians straight toward me. "Hades, you daughter snatcher!" she cried. "How dare you kidnap my Persephone?"

Before I could say a word, Persephone shouted, "Mom, stop! I came here with Hades because I wanted to. He didn't kidnap me!"

Demeter narrowed her eyes. "But Zeus said—"

"Zeus!" I growled, turning to my little brother. "You myth-o-maniac! Why would you make up such a ridiculous lie?"

When Zeus stepped forward, I saw that he'd grown a bit paunchy. They never showed his gut on *The Zeus Show.* "You know you kidnapped her, Hades," Zeus said with a smirk. "You might as well confess."

"Confess?" I felt my face growing hot. "I'm guilty of no crime!"

"I have a witness," said Zeus. "Helios, the sun god. He was in the sky at the time and he saw you grab her."

"He couldn't have," I said. "Because I didn't!"

Zeus shrugged. "It's your word against his."

My eyes searched the crowd of Olympians. "Where are you, Helios?" I called out. "Accuse me to my face!"

"Helios isn't here," said Zeus. "You know the sun can't ever leave the sky."

"That makes him a convenient witness, doesn't it?" I scoffed. "One who can't show up."

Zeus could never make the kidnapping charge stick. But why was he trying to keep me from marrying Persephone? Knowing him, the old myth-o-maniac had to have something up his sleeve.

"I'm staying here, Mom," Persephone was saying. "And Hades and I *are* getting married."

How glad I was to hear her words! "That's right," I said, stepping up to my goddess and putting my arm around her. "We're getting married. And," I added, hoping to change the direction of this conversation, "you're all invited to the wedding!"

"No, Hades!" cried Demeter. "You can't keep the goddess of spring imprisoned down here in this, this . . ." She gestured toward the asphodel, trying to find a word for it. "This muck," she said at last. "Persephone must walk upon the earth and make blossoms burst forth from the soil! She must—"

"Mom!" Persephone cut in. "Stop!"

Demeter turned to Zeus. "Tell them, Zeus. Tell them what you, the all-powerful Ruler of the Universe, promised me. That I could take Persephone home."

"That's what I said," Zeus agreed. "Demeter gets to take Persephone out of the Underworld."

"No, Dad!" said Persephone.

Dad? Zeus was Persephone's father? Aha! Maybe *that* was why Cerberus didn't like her. I shouldn't have been surprised, though. My little brother was really into building the Zeus Dynasty. He'd managed to become father or grandfather or uncle or brother to just about every god and goddess alive.

"Why do you always take her side, Dad?" Persephone was saying. "I am not six years old anymore! I want to have my own life!"

"Calm down, Persephone!" Zeus ordered. "I wasn't finished proclaiming yet. You interrupted me. Now, where was I? Oh, yes. Hades! Listen up! You can't accuse me of being unfair. No way! Because what I was about to say was that Demeter can take Persephone out of the Underworld, only if . . ."

Zeus paused, grinning wickedly. He waggled his eyebrows up and down.

Ohhh, this was such typical Zeus behavior, keeping us in suspense for as long as possible. How I wished this were *The Zeus Show*! Then, with a click of the remote, I could turn him off!

Zeus said *if* about a hundred times. Finally he finished: ". . . *if* she has not eaten any food that grows in the Underworld."

"What?" I cried. How had he managed to pick *this* of all the *ifs* in the universe? Then from somewhere behind me, I heard di Minos mutter, "And believe me, she hasn't!"

Aha, again! Di Minos had told Zeus about Persephone not wanting to eat any of the food down here. Now Zeus was using this as a way to keep me from marrying Persephone. Was I about to lose my bride over di Minos's asphodel strudel?

"Persephone, my dear," Zeus was saying, "no doubt the time has come for you to marry. But don't marry Hades. You need a worthy husband—one who lives in the fresh air and sunshine of Mount Olympus. My son Hermes, for example." He gave a nod in Hermes's direction. "He will make you an excellent spouse."

Fury rose up inside me as Hermes blew Persephone a kiss. The miserable little thief! He was trying to steal my bride!

But now I understood what Zeus was up to. He wanted Persephone to marry one of his sons so he could keep the goddess of spring, and spring itself, under his control. Well, I'd fight Zeus and Hermes both if I had to. They couldn't take Persephone away from me!

"My daughter would never eat the food of the dead!" Demeter declared. "The very name *Persephone* means 'picky eater.'"

"Mom?" said Persephone. "I have something to tell you."

"Come, Persephone," Demeter said. "Together, you and I shall return to earth and make it bloom!"

"Listen, Mom," said Persephone. "This morning—"

"Come, daughter!" Demeter called. "Return with me to the earth!"

At that moment, Cal stuck his head up above his swan-shaped hedge. "Excuse me?" he said. "I can clear this up."

All the Olympians and all the Underworldians grew quiet.

Zeus pulled himself up to his maximum height, which, without his platform sandals, wasn't all that tall. "And who would you be, hedge clipper?" he thundered.

"I'm Ascalaphus," he answered. "Gardener of the Underworld. You can call me Cal."

"And what do you have to say, lowly gardener?" asked Zeus.

"That she gets to stay," said Cal.

"What?" cried Zeus.

"I've been pruning these hedges since what passes for dawn down here," Cal began. "I saw Persephone cut through the field. Fresh asphodel blooms sprang up in her steps."

"Get to the point, clod buster!" cried Zeus.

"She got to the sample table early," said Cal. "The

waiters had just put out the first two bowls of what the king here calls 'starters.'"

"He means the asphodel chips and pomegranate dip," di Minos put in.

"That's them," said Cal.

"So?" thundered Zeus. He rattled his Bucket o' Bolts. "What of it, soil grubber? If you don't get to the point soon, I'll heave a thunderbolt your way!"

"She ate some, is what I'm saying," Cal said.

"Myth-o-maniac!" cried Demeter. "Persephone would never!"

"She did," Cal insisted. "I saw her do it through a hole in the hedge."

All eyes turned to Persephone.

"Speak, goddess!" said Zeus. "Did you eat the food of the dead?"

"Yes," said Persephone. "That's what I've been trying to tell you. The dip was excellent."

"Ha!" cried di Minos. "I knew you'd like it!"

Demeter threw herself to the ground. She started pounding it with her fists. "NOOOO!" she wailed. "I cannot lose my daughter to the Underworld!"

"Mom, get up," said Persephone through gritted teeth. "You are being so embarrassing!"

Demeter was way past caring about that. She raised herself, but only to her knees. "Nothing shall grow on the earth!" she cried, shaking a fist in the air. "Nothing! I swear it by the River Styx! As long as Persephone remains in the Underworld, THE EARTH SHALL WITHER!"

Chapter VIII

YAKKETY-YAK

The Underworld was usually a quiet place. Oh, once in a while some ghostly screams could be heard coming from the Punishment Fields of Tartarus, but that's nothing compared to the yelling and shouting that went on the day the Olympians invaded my kingdom to rescue Persephone.

Demeter's wails could be heard in the far reaches of my kingdom. Meg, Alec, Hypnos, Lightninger, Thunderer, the Hundred-Handed Ones, Campe, and thousands of curious ghosts ran over to the field in front of di Minos Pizza Parlor to see what in the Underworld was going on.

Zeus and Hera's son, Hephaestus, god of fire and smiths, began threatening Lightninger, saying he'd make his forge go dark.

A fistfight broke out between Zeus and Hera's other son, Ares, god of war, and Thunderer. The Cyclops ended up with a nasty black eye.

Lots of the Olympians held up signs that said things such as COME HOME, PERSEPHONE! and FLOWER POWER IS FOR THE EARTH!

When the Olympians' signs came out, the Hundred-Handed Ones disappeared for a few minutes. They quickly returned with hundreds of signs for the Underworldians to carry. They read: WE ♥ PERSEPHONE and OLYMPIANS, GO HOME! and WHO ASKED YOU?

Everyone was yelling at everyone else. It was *worse* than any nightmare I could imagine. In all the craziness, Persephone and I had been separated. I looked for her in the crowd. I finally spotted her standing with Tisi by Cal's swan-shaped hedge. Hermes was hovering above her, trying to impress her with aerial tricks, which he accomplished by fluttering the wings on his helmet and sandals. He called out, "Marry me, Persephone! I'll build you a golden palace up above the clouds! I'll fly you to the moon!"

Ohhh, how I longed to get my hands on that flapping opportunist!

Persephone looked sort of wilted and confused. Seeing her, I felt a sudden surge of love for my darling goddess of spring, and right then, I knew what I had to do.

I hurried around to where Tisi had parked my chariot. To my relief, my Helmet of Darkness was still on the backseat. I grabbed the helmet and jammed it onto my head. Instantly, I vanished. Unseen, I rushed back into the crowd. I ran until I reached Persephone. "My darling!" I whispered.

"Hades?" Persephone turned, looking for me. "Where are you?"

"I'm at your side," I said. "But you can't see me."

"No kidding," said Persephone. "What's going on? Are you really Hades? I can't take many more surprises."

"Tisi," I said. "Tell her it's me."

"It's Hades," said Tisi. "Invisible King of the

Underworld." And she explained about the helmet, and how it made me and anything I held invisible.

"Elope with me, Persephone," I said. "I'll carry you away from here. No one will see us! I know this great little spot up in Athens where we can get married."

"Hades!" Persephone's eyes grew wide. "You don't mean Ari's Speedy Wedding Chapel?"

"I do, my darling," I confessed. "I know it's sort of cheesy, and that you don't want a spur-of-the-moment wedding, but—"

"Stop, Hades!" said Persephone.

I stopped. Persephone held out her hand. I took it and gave it an invisible squeeze. Together, we looked around us at the sign wielders and the brawlers and the yellers and the screamers. We looked at Demeter, who was still lying on the ground, kicking her feet, pounding the dirt with her fists, and weeping.

"I wanted big and splashy," Persephone said at last. "But I never imagined *this*! Right now, cheesy and spur-of-the-moment sounds perfect!"

I swept Persephone up in my arms, and she, too, vanished from sight.

"Come on, Tisi," I shouted as I ran for the chariot. "You can be our witness!"

Persephone and I waited invisibly outside di Minos Pizza, while Tisi took the chariot and rushed back to the palace. There was no way she was going to let us get married without *some* style—even in a tacky mortal wedding chapel—so she insisted on going back for Persephone's gown and my toga-tux. She also picked up her sister Furies, who would have been *furious* if they'd missed the wedding.

When Tisi returned, I stepped into the driver's seat and took off my Helmet of Darkness. There was no need to be invisible now. I drove us all up to earth.

The sun had set by the time we reached Athens. The streets were filled with revelers, out having a good time in the city. I found a parking spot on a side street. The five of us walked eagerly toward Ari's Speedy Wedding Chapel, Tisi with two large garment bags over her arm.

A long line of mortal couples waiting to get married snaked from the door of Ari's out onto the street.

"Look at that line!" Persephone groaned. "We'll have to wait for hours!"

"I don't think so," said Tisi. She and her sisters walked calmly to the front of the line. They raised their arms over their heads, extended their claws, and—*thwap!*—unfurled their huge, black, leathery wings, all at the same time.

Instantly, the line of mortals vanished.

"How about that?" said Meg, refolding her wings.

"Your turn!" Alec told Persephone.

The five of us walked into the now deserted chapel. An ancient mortal in a shabby white robe opened his mouth to greet us. But when he saw us, he did a double take and froze. For a moment, I was afraid he'd died of fright and there would be no one to marry us.

"Ari?" said Tisi. "Hello? Anybody home?"

"Me," managed Ari, who turned out only to be stunned.

"This is Persephone, goddess of spring," Tisi told the mortal.

"And Hades, Lord of the Dead," said Meg.

"They would like to get married," said Alec. *"Now."*

"Of course!" Old Ari rose shakily to his feet. His voice trembled as he said, "It is beyond my wildest dreams to imagine that I, a humble mortal, would one day perform the wedding ceremony for you, Lord Hades! And you, Goddess Persephone. It is—"

"Time to start," Alec cut in. *"Right now!"*

"Of course!" said Ari. "Follow me! In just ten minutes, you shall be man and—uh, I mean, god and—I mean, married."

We trooped after Ari as he tottered into the actual chapel, a small circular room with columns running around it. Garlands of wilted greenery with droopy flowers were draped between the columns. Persephone hurried over, and at her touch, the greenery perked up. The flowers opened into gorgeous spring blossoms.

She smiled. "That's more like it." Then she and the Furies scurried off to the bride's chamber to get dressed.

Ari took me into the groom's chamber, and I

began struggling into my toga-tux. It wasn't easy. Ari tried to help me tie the strip of polka-dotted silk around my neck, but his hands shook so badly that, in the end, I had to tie it myself. The whole time I was dressing, Ari went on and on about what a great honor it was for him to marry us.

At last we walked back out to the chapel. I was nervous, but I wasn't shaking half as much as Ari. I was worried about him. Would he last through the ceremony? That's the trouble with mortals—they're so . . . mortal. You never know when they'll drop dead on you.

Two musicians appeared then, and began strumming their lyres. That seemed the signal to begin. With some difficulty, Ari walked up two small steps and turned around to face me.

Now Meg and Alec started down the aisle wearing slinky silver gowns. Tisi, the maid of honor, followed them, decked out in gold.

The music changed to *The Wedding March*. Now my bride started down the aisle, her gown shimmering with pearls. Her face was nearly hidden by her enormous bouquet, but I could see her smiling through her veil. She stopped beside me, and took my arm.

Ari cleared his throat. "We are here to unite this couple in marriage," he said. "Marriage is a big step—especially for you immortals, because when you vow to stay together forever, it really means *forever*."

"Ari, cut to the chase," hissed Alec.

"Of course!" said Ari. "Does anyone present know of any reason why Persephone, goddess of spring, and Hades, Lord of the Dead, should not be united in marriage? If so, speak now, or forever hold—"

At that moment, I heard voices shouting and dogs barking, and someone yelled out, "Stop the wedding!"

"Oh, no!" cried Meg.

I whirled around to see who could have said such a thing. There at the entrance to the wedding chapel stood *my* mother, the take-charge Titaness, Rhea. Oops! I'd forgotten to invite her to my wedding!

Uncle Shiner stood next to her. He held a leash, and at the end of it was my very own underdog!

"Good dog, Cerberus!" said Uncle Shiner. "It appears as though you tracked your master down just in the nick of time."

Cerbie had tracked me down? But why? Cerbie wagged his tail and let out a chorus of happy squeals at seeing me again. He tried to run to me, but Uncle Shiner held his leash tight.

"Hades, I have something of the utmost importance to tell you," Uncle Shiner said. "It will change the way you view your current situation, I promise you."

What was he talking about? What was going on? My head was spinning.

"Persephone has committed an unscrupulous act of which you are unaware," Uncle Shiner continued. "She—"

"Stop!" I yelled. "Mom! What are you and Uncle Shiner doing here?"

"Your Granny Gaia sent me," said my mom. "She's very upset. And I am, too. Is this how you solve your problems, Hades? By running away from them?"

"Not usually," I said. "But I thought—"

I gulped. I remembered the bone-rattling earthquakes our Granny Gaia, a.k.a. Mother Earth, had started the last time she got upset with me.

"You didn't think, Hades," Mom said. "That's the trouble. And you, Persephone! Shame on you!"

"What did I do?" asked Persephone.

"You heard your mother swear an unbreakable oath on the waters of the River Styx that as long as you stay in the Underworld, the earth shall wither," said Mom.

Persephone nodded. "I heard her," she said, "but I thought—"

"But you thought," Mom cut in, "that you'd marry Hades and become Queen of the Underworld anyway."

Persephone shrugged. "I guess."

Mom shook her head. "You, Gaia's own great-granddaughter!"

Persephone sat down heavily on the steps of the chapel, resting her chin on her hands. Her dazzling smile had vanished.

"We need to go down to the Underworld and get everything sorted out," Mom said. She turned to

Tisi. "If you three can fly back down, there'll be room for Shiner and me and these"—she held up the big shopping bags that she always carried with her—"in Hades's chariot."

"Not a problem," said Tisi.

"We fly it every day," said Meg.

"Here," said Mom. She picked up Cerberus and handed him to Alec. "Take the dog."

"Got him," said Alec. "We're out of here. *Now!*"

All three of Cerberus's faces looked confused as he flew off with the Furies.

"Oh, rats," murmured Ari. He looked so disappointed at this turn of events that I gave him an extra-large tip as I left the chapel. Outside, I saw that a new line of mortals wanting to get married had already formed around the block. It didn't look as if Ari would get much sleep that night.

Persephone and I followed Mom and Uncle Shiner back to the chariot in grim silence. I felt awful. I'd been ordered back to my kingdom by my own mother, like some toddler, to "sort things out" with a gang of hostile Olympians. It didn't look as if Persephone could ever be my bride, because if she lived in the Underworld, nothing would grow on earth. And why had Uncle Shiner turned against me? I didn't have a clue. But worst of all, they'd used my own dog to track me down.

That really hurt.

Chapter IX

STATIC

It was midmorning by the time I drove my chariot back into the Asphodel Fields with Mom taking up practically the whole front seat. The Olympians and the Underworldians were still quarreling. But when they saw my mom, everyone stopped shouting.

Hera was the first to find her voice. "Mother!" she exclaimed. "How good to see you!"

"You, too, dear," said Mom, stepping out of the chariot. "But enough chitchat. I'm here on business. I've been sent by Mother Earth. Listen, Demeter, your Granny Gaia isn't one bit happy with you."

While Mom scolded Demeter, I hurried over to

Alec. Cerberus saw me coming and ran to greet me, smothering me with doggie kisses. I couldn't blame my pooch for tracking me down. He'd only wanted to find his master. Cerberus trotted after me back to where Mom was lecturing Demeter.

"Mother Earth doesn't like it when the mortals' fields dry up and they can't grow their crops," Mom was explaining. "The mortals begin to go hungry. And when they're hungry, they get cranky. And when they're cranky, they don't send Mother Earth any decent sacrifices. Are you getting this, Demeter? Things can't go on this way!"

"But I can't summon the good feelings I need to make the earth bloom," Demeter whined. "Not when my own daughter is wilting down in this pit."

I wished she wouldn't call my kingdom a pit.

"Right!" Zeus called out. "And Persephone? You don't want to marry a god who can't even tie a bow tie, do you?"

Oops! I'd forgotten that I was still dressed in my toga-tux.

"I say we get Persephone out of here!" said Zeus. "I say—"

"Put a sock in it, Zeusie," said Mom. "I want to hear what Demeter has to say."

Demeter sniffed. "If Persephone comes back to earth with me again, I shall be happy, and the earth shall burst forth with wheat and corn!"

"Yes!" cried the Olympians. "Demeter must get her daughter back."

"But I don't want to go!" Persephone folded her arms across her chest. "I want to stay here in the Underworld and marry Hades!"

"That's what I want, too," I added.

"Yes! Let them have their wedding!" cried the Underworldians.

The Olympians started chanting: *"Hey-hey! Hey-ho! Persephone has got to go!"*

And the Underworldians chanted back: *"Ho-ho! Hey-hey! Persephone has got to stay!"*

"Whoo, boy," said Mom. "There must be some way to make everybody happy." She turned to me. "Hades, have you a courthouse in your kingdom?"

I nodded.

"Good," said Mom. "Let's go there. I always carry my judging robe for just such an occasion." She patted one of her shopping bags.

"Hold it," said King di Minos. "It's my courthouse. I'm the judge!"

"Not today, di Minos," Mom said. "I'll be the judge of this. And take off that silly crown. You haven't been king of anything for centuries."

Di Minos grumbled and took off the crown. But I knew it would be back on his head the next time I saw him.

Everyone began cutting across the Asphodel Fields then, heading for the courthouse. I saw that Persephone had already started walking with the Furies, so I drove over in my chariot with Cerbie.

At the courthouse, Mom slipped on her black robe and squeezed behind the high judging desk. She barely fit. The rest of us found seats on the benches usually occupied by ghosts. I took the center aisle seat in the first row. Cerberus sat down at my feet. I turned around and searched the crowd. At last I found Persephone. She and the Furies were sitting near the back of the courtroom. I smiled and held up my crossed fingers for luck. Persephone did the same.

"Let's begin." Mom banged the gavel. "Here is our problem: Demeter wants Persephone to come home so she can be happy enough to make things grow on earth. But Persephone wants to stay in the Underworld and marry Hades." Mom looked out into the courtroom. "Does anyone have anything to say in favor of Demeter's position?"

"I do!" Zeus jumped to his feet.

Mom began banging her gavel, but Zeus yelled over the banging.

"As Ruler of the Universe, I say Demeter gets her way!" he shouted. "Okay, that's it. We're finished here. Case dismissed!"

Mom gave an extra-loud bang. "Zeus, sit!" she ordered. "This isn't *The Zeus Show*. This is a trial. I want to hear what everyone has to say and make an informed judgement. Is that all right with you?"

"Not really," Zeus muttered, but he sat back down.

"Does anyone *else* have anything to say in favor of Demeter?" Mom asked.

To my surprise, Uncle Shiner stood up. "I have."

Everyone began whispering. No one had expected anyone from the Underworld to take Demeter's side. Uncle Shiner walked to the front of the courtroom. I wondered what I could have done to make the Cyclops turn against me.

"I call the god Cupid to the stand," Uncle Shiner said.

As Cupid walked past us to the witness seat, one of Cerberus's mouths snapped at him.

"Hey!" cried Cupid, jumping away. "That dog is a menace, man! He shouldn't be in a courtroom!"

"Hades, could you *please* control your dog?" asked Mom.

"Absolutely." I gave Cerbie a look, and he sat back down as Cupid took the witness stand.

"Do you swear to tell the truth and to forgo all myth-o-mania?" asked Mom.

"If I have to," said Cupid.

"You are the god of love, are you not?" Uncle Shiner asked Cupid.

"That's me," said Cupid.

"And you occasionally shoot gods and mortals

with what you call 'love arrows,'" said Uncle Shiner. "Is this correct?"

"That's my main job," said Cupid.

"Exactly what happens when, let's say, a god is struck with such a love arrow?" asked Uncle Shiner.

"He falls in love, man." Cupid smirked. "Head-over-heels in love with the first goddess or mortal he looks at after he's been hit."

"I see," said Uncle Shiner. "Now, Cupid, are you acquainted with the goddess of spring?"

"Am I what?" he asked.

"Do you know Persephone?" said Uncle Shiner.

"Persephone? Yeah, I know her," said Cupid.

"Did she ever ask you to shoot an arrow at anyone sitting in this courtroom?" said Uncle Shiner.

"I'm not ratting on Persephone, man," said Cupid.

"Answer the question, Cupid," said Mom. "And tell the truth."

"Okay, okay. Persephone set it up for me to shoot *him*." Cupid pointed right at me!

Loud murmurs broke out in the courtroom.

Why would my darling Persephone ask Cupid to shoot me? It didn't make sense. It couldn't be true!

But Cupid wasn't finished. "I hid in the bushes while Persephone and Hades had a picnic," he continued. "Then I took aim and—*zing!* I got him!"

I turned in my seat to look at Persephone. I thought she might have jumped to her feet to yell that it wasn't true. But she only glared at Cupid. I was stunned. Had Persephone tricked me into falling in love with her?

"But I just about got ripped apart by Hades's mutt," Cupid was saying. "That dog needs a muzzle, man. No, make that *three* muzzles."

I managed to grab Cerberus's collar just as he was leaping up to have another go at Cupid.

"And Persephone still owes me for the job, too," Cupid finished up.

Persephone had offered Cupid money to shoot me? My head was spinning.

"Cupid," said Uncle Shiner, "will you kindly show us one of your love arrows?"

The god of love reached into his quiver and pulled out a small golden arrow. I was sad to see that it looked exactly like the one I'd pulled from the back of my neck.

Uncle Shiner turned toward Mom. "You have heard how Persephone hired Cupid to carry out the cold-blooded shooting of the unsuspecting Hades," he said. "This is treachery. This is deceit. And this is why Hades must not go through with the wedding."

Everyone in the courthouse burst out talking at once. So *this* was what Uncle Shiner had been trying to tell me!

Mom banged her gavel. "Order in the court!" she called. "Shiner, do you have a theory as to why the goddess of spring might have hired Cupid to shoot Hades? What was her motive?"

"Possibly she wanted to marry him to get away from her mother," said Uncle Shiner. "But I suspect that her main motivation was to become Queen of the Underworld."

Everyone started buzzing again, and Mom started banging her gavel.

Had Persephone done all this to be queen? I felt as if I'd just been jabbed in the heart.

Mom looked at me. "Well, Hades? What do you have to say?"

I opened my mouth, but nothing came out.

"Shiner's interrogation sheds new light on the case," Mom said. "Do you want to call off the wedding, Hades?"

I sat frozen to the spot. I couldn't say a word.

"Because if you do," she went on, "just say the word, and Demeter will take Persephone back to earth immediately."

"Yes!" Demeter yelled out. "Call it off, Hades!"

Mom banged her gavel to silence Demeter. "Order!" she said. Then she added, "Hades is too shaken to speak, so I think the best thing for me to do is to call off the—"

"Wait!" cried Hera.

Mom peered down at her. "What is it, Hera?"

Hera stood. "As you know, Mother, I am the goddess of marriage."

"Hera, is this remotely related to the case?" asked Mom.

"It is," Hera said. "As the protector of marriage, it is my duty to make sure that this wedding isn't being called off too soon."

"Hera!" barked Zeus. "Don't go there!"

"Shush." Hera waved at Zeus, but kept her eyes on Mom. "You asked whether anyone had anything to say in favor of Demeter's case," she said. "But you haven't asked if anyone has anything to say in favor of Persephone's."

"You're right," said Mom. "I've been a little hasty." She looked around the courtroom. "Well? Does anyone have anything to say?"

"I do!" came Tisi's voice from the back of the courtroom.

"All right, Tisi," said Mom. "To be fair, you may have your say. But it's been a long day, so you'll have to do it first thing tomorrow morning. Hypnos?" Her eyes scanned the courtroom. "There you are. Wake up! Prepare the Titan Suite in Motel Styx. I'll be staying there tonight." She banged her gavel. "Everyone report back here tomorrow morning at IX o'clock. Court dismissed!"

Chapter X

DIAL "M" FOR MOM

As soon as Mom left the courtroom, Uncle Shiner pushed his way through the crowd to me. Taking me gently by the elbow, he pulled me outside. He walked me to my chariot, and drove Cerbie and me back to Villa Pluto.

With all that had happened, I was in shock. I couldn't speak. Uncle Shiner didn't say anything for a while, either. But at last he said, "Hades, I am sorry for the pain this has caused you."

I nodded.

"I thought you should know the truth," he added. "I hope you won't hold it against me."

I shook my head.

Uncle Shiner dropped me off at the front entrance of Villa Pluto, saying he'd take Harley and Davidson on to the stable. I picked up my helmet from the backseat, and trudged slowly up the walk.

I went into the den and flopped down in my La-Z-God. Cerberus stretched out at my feet. My head was buzzing with all that I'd heard in court. I needed time to put my thoughts in order. Had Persephone really hired Cupid to shoot me just so she could become Queen of the Underworld? I still loved her like crazy. But was my love real? What if I only loved Persephone because I'd looked at her directly after being shot by Cupid's little arrow? If I'd looked up and seen Tisi, would I now be head over heels in love with a Fury? Whoa! That was a scary thought.

I heard voices outside in the hallway. I leaped up, and jammed on my Helmet of Darkness. I disappeared. I picked up Cerbie, and he vanished, too. And just in time. The door swung open. In came Persephone, followed by all three Furies.

"Hades?" Persephone called. "Are you here?"

I didn't answer.

"Oh, I wish I could find him," Persephone said, collapsing onto the couch. "He looked so upset at the courthouse, poor dear."

"You can't blame him," said Tisi. "Shiner *was* a little rough."

"Ohhhh, wait until I get my hands on that meddling Cyclops!" Persephone clenched her fists. "I can't believe he accused me of such treachery!"

A knock sounded. The door to the den swung open again, and in came Demeter. Was I ever glad I was invisible!

"Mom!" exclaimed Persephone. "What are you doing here?"

"Looking for you," said Demeter.

"So what else is new?" muttered Persephone.

Demeter made a beeline for the couch and sat down beside her daughter. "Persephone, we have to talk," she said.

"No!" cried Persephone. "I'm not talking to you ever again! You have ruined my life. Totally! I don't want to come back to earth and be your little gardening buddy. I want to have a life! I want to—"

Persephone stopped. "What's that hissing noise?" She looked from her mother to the Furies. "Ahhhhh!" she cried.

The Furies stood together before Persephone with their arms crossed. The snakes on their heads were writhing and hissing furiously.

"Yikes!" yelped Persephone. "Why are they doing that?"

"You're not being very nice to your mother, Persephone," said Tisi.

"Not nice at all," said Meg.

"Be nice," said Alec. *"Now!"*

The snakes began darting at Persephone, their fang-filled mouths stretched wide.

Persephone drew back. "But you see how Mom is!" she cried. "She sticks to me like an octopus clinging to a rock! Like moss clinging to a tree! Like an eagle, clinging to its prey! She can't stand it when I'm out of her sight! She—"

"She loves you," Tisi put in.

"She wants you to be happy," said Meg.

"She wants to talk to you," said Alec. "So talk. *Now.*"

"Okay," Persephone managed. She turned toward Demeter. "Sorry about that."

The snakes backed off a bit.

Demeter glanced up at the Furies. "Thank you," she said. Then she turned back to Persephone. "Am I really as clingy as all that?" she asked.

Persephone shrugged. "Sort of."

"I had no idea," said Demeter. "I thought mothers and daughters were supposed to be close. Very, very, very close."

"Close," said Persephone. "But not 'very, very, very.'"

"I see." Demeter nodded thoughtfully. "Well, I shall try to let go of you, Persephone. A little bit at a time."

"That's a start, Mom." Persephone smiled.

"Now, tell me the truth, Persephone," Demeter went on. "Did you really hire Cupid to shoot Hades with a love arrow?"

I held my breath, waiting. What would Persephone say?

To my great sorrow, she nodded and said, "Yes."

Now I had no more room for doubt. Cupid's story was true. Persephone had tricked me.

"But why?" asked Demeter.

Persephone sighed. "It's a long story."

"Tell it to your mother," said Tisi.

"Start at the beginning," said Meg.

"Start *now*," said Alec.

"Okay," said Persephone. "The first time I saw Hades, he was driving his steeds across a field outside of Athens. He looked so . . . I don't know . . . so strong, so godly, so . . . *in charge*."

I felt my face growing warm. I was blushing! It was a good thing no one could see me.

"I waved him down so I could meet him," Persephone went on. "I really liked him, but I was afraid he'd think I was just some ditzy little junior goddess. I figured he'd like me if he got to know me, so I hitched a ride to the Underworld so that we could spend more time together."

Demeter looked puzzled. "Why do you suppose Zeus told me that Hades kidnapped you?"

"Oh, you know Dad hardly ever tells the truth," said Persephone. "He was trying to make Hades look bad so Hermes would look good, and I'd want to marry him." She made a face.

"Anyway, when I showed up in the Underworld, Hades was mad at me, and I knew he wouldn't give me a chance. All he could think about was getting rid of me." She glanced up at the Furies. "So when you tricked me and took me back to my mother, and then felt all sorry about it. . . ." Persephone smiled. "That's when I thought of getting Cupid to help me out a little."

"So you did it for love." Meg sighed. "That is so romantic!"

"I love Hades," Persephone said. "But after what Cupid said on the witness stand today, I don't think he'll ever believe me." She sighed sadly.

I wanted to rip off the Helmet of Darkness. I wanted to swoop Persephone up in my arms. But one thing stopped me.

What if this was just another one of Persephone's sneaky tricks?

The next morning, Mom's gavel sounded. *Bang!*

I sat in the front row of the courtroom as before, with Cerberus at my feet.

"The court will come to order!" Mom said.

"Tisi? Stand and present the case for Persephone."

Tisi rose. "Thank you, Judge Rhea," she said. "I'd like to call Cupid to the stand for a cross-examination."

"Aw, man!" the little god said. But he made his way once more to the witness seat.

"Cupid," said Tisi, "what is it that gives your love arrows their power?"

"You think I'm going to tell you my secret formula?" said Cupid. "Not a chance!"

Tisi shrugged. "Well, you can't blame me for trying," she said. "Now tell me, Cupid, does a love arrow make whoever is shot with it fall in love forever?"

"Forever?" said Cupid. "Are you kidding? No, man. That would put me out of business fast."

"Then how long does the love last?" asked Tisi. "A year? A month?"

Cupid shook his head. "A good solid hit lasts three days, tops."

"I see," said Tisi. "And how long ago did you shoot Hades?"

"I don't know exactly." Cupid shrugged.

"But more than three days ago," said Tisi.

"Sure," said Cupid. "Yeah, it's been at least a week."

Tisi spun around to face me.

"The power from Cupid's arrow wore off days ago, Hades," she said. "You are no longer under its spell. So my question to you is, do you love Persephone? Because if you love her now, then you love her for real."

It was so quiet in that courtroom you could have heard an asphodel leaf drop. All eyes were on me. Beads of drosis broke out on my forehead.

Did I love Persephone?

Chapter XI

SPEAK UP

Somehow I managed to rise to my feet. I turned, looking for Persephone. She wasn't sitting where she'd been the day before, in the back of the packed courtroom with the Furies. Where was she?

"Do you love Persephone?" Tisi asked again.

"Do you, Hades?" called Meg. "Do you?"

"Speak up *now*!" said Alec.

"I—I," I said, wiping the drosis from my brow. "I—uh, I . . ."

Finally I found Persephone. She was sitting next to her mother! That was a switch.

I tried again to speak, but before I could get my words out, Zeus leaped to his feet.

"Persephone!" he cried. "Forget Hades! Listen to him, mumbling and bumbling. He can't even talk! Check out Hermes over here! He's crazy about you. And he gets invited to all the best parties!"

That did it! I found my voice.

"Persephone!" I said loud and clear. "I love you!"

"Oh, I knew it!" cried Meg.

"Cupid's arrow might have started things off," I continued. "But now? It's the real thing."

Persephone broke into a great big smile, and everyone from the Underworld exploded into cheers and whistles. Lots of the Olympians did, too. From somewhere in the courtroom, chanting started: *"Wed-ding! Wed-ding! Wed-ding!"*

I looked at Demeter. She wasn't cheering or chanting, of course. But she hadn't thrown herself to the ground in a fit, either. I took that to be a good sign.

Mom kept pounding her gavel, but even so, it took quite a while for the noise to die down. "Thank you, Tisi," she said at last. "And thank you, Hades, my firstborn." She gave me her best Mom smile. "We have solved that problem," she said. "Now, on to the others."

Others? What problems could she mean?

"Demeter, you swore upon the River Styx," said Mom. "You vowed that as long as Persephone remained in the Underworld, nothing would grow upon the earth. As you know, oaths sworn on the Styx are unbreakable."

Right after she said that, the whole Underworld began to shake and rumble.

"That was a message from Granny Gaia," said Mom. "She's not going to sit still while you let all the growing things on earth wither and die. Got that, Demeter?"

"But what can I do?" wailed Demeter. "I can't make plants grow on earth if I'm miserable. And without Persephone, I'll be miserable."

Persephone put an arm around her mother's shoulder. "I don't want you to be miserable," she said. "But I don't want to be miserable, either. And without Hades, I'll be miserable. I can't come back to earth with you."

"You couldn't, even if you wanted to, my dear," said Mom.

"What do you mean?" said Persephone. "Why not?"

"Because Zeus decreed that if you ate the food of the dead, you would have to remain in the Underworld," Mom reminded her.

Zeus popped up. "Say you'll marry Hermes!" he shouted. "And I'll take back my decree!"

"Down, Zeus!" said Mom. "You know you can't take back decrees."

"But Persephone hardly ate anything," Demeter protested. "That gardener said she only nibbled a few chips."

"Shhh! Both of you!" said Mom. "Let me think." She drummed her fingers on her desk. After a moment, she pointed at Cal, who was sitting in the middle of the crowded courtroom. "Take the stand, will you, Ascalaphus?"

Cal ambled toward the witness seat. He sat down.

"Do you swear to tell the truth and forgo all myth-o-mania?" she asked.

Cal nodded. "That I do."

"How many chips did you see Persephone eat?" Rhea asked him.

"One is the number when it comes to chips," said Cal. "But another number comes to mind if you consider the dipping."

"What are you saying, Cal?" asked Rhea. "Spell it out for the court."

"What I'm saying," said Cal, "is that Persephone took a chip, dipped it and bit off the part with the pomegranate dip. Then she put that very same chip, only smaller now, into the dip again and took another bite. All she had left then was a crumb of the chip, but she poked it into the pomegranate dip and scooped up all she could." Cal shrugged. "Not that there's anything wrong with it, especially if everyone's family, but the truth is, Persephone triple dipped."

Mom's eyebrows went up. "Persephone? A triple dip?"

Persephone shrugged and smiled. "I told you. The dip was outstanding."

"One chip, three dips," said Mom. She thought for a moment. "All right, here is my decision." She pounded her gavel for emphasis. "Hades, you may marry Persephone."

I grinned as cheers rose in the courthouse.

"Persephone? You may rule as Queen of the Underworld," Mom went on. "But it won't be your full-time job."

"What do you mean?" asked Persephone.

"You'll spend the greater part of each year up on earth performing your duties as goddess of spring and helping your mother," said Mom. "But for every time you dipped that chip into the pomegranate dip, you will live one month of the year in the Underworld."

"What am I going to be, some sort of time-share goddess?" said Persephone.

"Exactly," said Mom. "Can you live with that?"

Persephone frowned. "But one month for every dip is only three months a year!"

"Correct," said Mom. "Take it or leave it."

"I'll take it," Persephone said quickly. "But only if Hades can come up to earth now and then to visit me."

Mom shrugged. "What's to stop him?"

Persephone broke into a smile.

"Okay by you, Hades?" said Mom.

"It's fine," I said. And it was. I loved Persephone, and I wanted her to be my queen. But I'd been worried about having her around *all* the time. Especially for Cerbie's sake. This was a perfect arrangement.

But would it work for Demeter?

All eyes found her now as she rose to her feet.

"I swore on the River Styx. I cannot take back my oath," Demeter declared. "While Persephone is in the Underworld, I shall be on strike as goddess of agriculture. But," she added, "the earth can survive for three months without my tending." She looked upward. "If I'm wrong, may Granny Gaia strike us with an earthquake!"

We all waited for the earth to start trembling, but it didn't.

"You've made your point," said Mom.

Demeter nodded. "For three months of each year, the trees shall lose their leaves, the grass shall wither, and no crops shall grow," she said. "I will call this time . . . winter."

"But what will you do during the winter?" asked Mom.

"I shall take time off," Demeter said. "I will call this time . . . vacation."

"But where will you go?" asked Mom.

Now, for the first time since she'd come to the Underworld, Demeter smiled. "I'm going to get myself a little bungalow someplace warm. I won't work too hard, just hard enough to make sure it's never winter there. I shall call this place . . . Florida."

"Sounds like a plan, Demeter," Mom said. She looked around the courtroom. "If there is anything more to say, say it now."

To my horror, Uncle Shiner stood up again.

"Just one more thing," he said. "We have heard from Hades that his love for Persephone is real. But we have not heard from Persephone. I, for one, would like to hear her declare that she loves my nephew."

"Well, Persephone?" Mom said. "What do you say to that?"

Persephone popped up and said, "I love Hades!"

Everyone cheered now, Underworldians and Olympians alike.

"I loved him the minute I saw him," she went on.

I felt my face turning red. And this time, everyone could see.

Uncle Shiner smiled. "That's what I'd hoped to hear," he said. "My best wishes to the bride and groom!"

The room filled with cheering again. And I knew that the old Cyclops had been looking out for me all along.

Tisi sprang up. "I realize that this is short notice," she began, "but since you Olympians are here, and probably won't be coming back any time soon, we'd like to invite you to the wedding of Hades and Persephone which will take place at Villa Pluto tonight at VII o'clock."

Tonight? Our wedding? This was the first I'd heard of it.

But that was fine by me, Hades.

Epilogue

I know the story of *Phone Home, Persephone!* by heart, so I wrote it myself, without the help of any ghostwriters. When I finished, I asked my good Titan buddy Hyperion to read it. Not that the old cattle rancher is any judge of literature, but a writer always likes to have a little feedback before a book goes to press.

I was sitting beside the Pool of Lethe one afternoon, thinking and thumbing through *The Big Fat Book of Greek Myths* when I saw Hyperion's old chariot heading my way.

The Titan reined in his steeds and jumped out of

his chariot. He had my manuscript pages in his hand. "Boy, howdy, Hades!" he said. "This is a heck of a good story about you and Queen Persephone."

I smiled. This was exactly the kind of feedback I'd been looking for.

"But you ended it too quick, boy," Hyperion went on. "What happened at the wedding?"

I thought back. "Well, I asked Uncle Shiner to be my best man. Cerberus whimpered through the whole ceremony, but believe it or not, Demeter didn't shed a tear."

"Who married ya'all?" Hyperion asked. "Di Minos?"

"No way," I said. "Not long after we left Ari's Speedy Wedding Chapel, old Ari dropped dead. So Tisi arranged for his ghost to marry us. It was a great wedding, and afterward, at the reception, Shades of Purple played, and everyone danced." I sighed happily, remembering. "Quite a few romances sprang up that night. I thought maybe my little brother Po might be the next to marry, the way he danced all night with Medusa."

"Medusa?" Hyperion scrunched up his face.

"Isn't she that double-ugly snake-haired Gorgon chick?"

I stared at Hyperion. "Is that who you think Medusa is?" I asked him. I picked up *The Big Fat Book of Greek Myths* and started reading:

Medusa was a Gorgon, a winged monster with hissing serpents for hair. Anyone who looked upon her face was turned to stone.

Perseus, bold son of the brave and mighty Zeus, waited until Medusa fell asleep, then cut off her horrible head.

"Yep, that's her," Hyperion said. "Boy, howdy! Makes you glad that fellah Perseus whacked off her head!"

"But he didn't!" I said. "That's a lie! That's just what my myth-o-maniac brother Zeus wants everyone to think. But there's more to Medusa's story than that. Much more!"

Hyperion broke into a grin. "Sounds like you've just found the subject for your next book, partner."

"You're right," I said. I thought for a moment, then added, "Here's what I'll call it—*Say Cheese, Medusa!*"

"Call it whatever you want," said Hyperion. "But write it fast, will you, buddy? If there's one thing I can't stand, it's waiting to read a book."

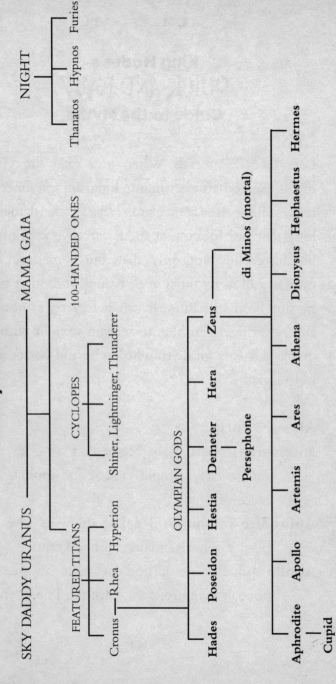

King Hades's
QUICK-AND-EASY
Family Tree of the Gods

SKY DADDY URANUS ——————— MAMA GAIA

NIGHT
— Thanatos Hypnos Furies

100-HANDED ONES

CYCLOPES
— Shiner, Lightninger, Thunderer

FEATURED TITANS
— Cronus — Rhea   Hyperion

OLYMPIAN GODS
Hades Poseidon Hestia Demeter Hera Zeus
                          Persephone

Aphrodite Apollo Artemis Ares Athena di Minos (mortal) Dionysus Hephaestus Hermes
Cupid

King Hades's
QUICK-AND-EASY
Guide to the Myths

Let's face it, mortals. When you read the Greek myths, you sometimes run into long, unpronounceable names like *Ascalaphus* and *Hephaestus*—names so long that just looking at them can give you a great big headache. Not only that, but sometimes you mortals call us by our Greek names, and other times by our Roman names. It can get pretty confusing. But never fear! I'm here to set you straight with my quick-and-easy guide to who's who and what's what in the myths.

Alec: see **Furies**.

ambrosia [am-BRO-zha]: food that we gods must eat to stay young and good-looking for eternity.

Aphrodite [af-ruh-DIE-tee]: goddess of love and beauty. The Romans call her **Venus**.

Apollo [uh-POL-oh]: god of light, music, and poetry; Artemis's twin brother. The Romans couldn't come up with anything better, so they call him **Apollo**, too.

Ares [AIR-eez]: god of war. The Romans call him **Mars**.

Artemis [AR-tuh-miss]: goddess of the hunt and the moon, Apollo's twin sister. The Romans call her **Diana**.

Ascalaphus [ass-KAL-uh-fuss]: gardener of the Underworld; Cal for short.

Asphodel [ASS-fo-del] **Fields**: the large region of the Underworld where nothing grows except for a weedy gray-green plant; home to the ghosts of those who, in life, were not so good, but not so bad.

Athena [a-THEE-nuh]: goddess of three w's: wisdom, weaving, and war. The Romans call her **Minerva**.

Athens [ATH-enz]: major city in Greece.

Campe [CAM-pee]: giantess and Underworld Jail Keep.

Cerberus [SIR-buh-rus]: my fine, three-headed pooch, guard dog of the Underworld.

Charon [CARE-un]: river-taxi driver; ferries the

living and the dead across the River Styx.

Cronus [CROW-nus]: my dad, a truly sneaky Titan, who once ruled the universe. The Romans called him **Saturn**.

Cupid [KYOO-pid]: god of love; Cupid is his Roman name. The Greeks call him **Eros**.

Cyclops [SIGH-klops]: a one-eyed giant. Lightninger, Shiner, and Thunderer, children of Gaia and Uranus, and uncles to us gods, are three **cyclopes** [sigh-KLO-peez].

Demeter [duh-MEE-ter]: my sister, goddess of agriculture and total gardening nut. The Romans call her **Ceres**.

di Minos [dih ME-nus]: better known as King Minos, son of Zeus, who set him up as a judge of the ghosts in the Underworld.

Dionysus [die-uh-NIE-sus]: god of wine and good-time party guy. The Romans call him **Bacchus**.

discus [DIS-kus]: a disk thrown in athletic competition; ancestor of the Frisbee.

drosis [DRO-sis]: short for **theoexidrosis**

[thee-oh-ex-ih-DRO-sis], old Greek-speak for "violent god sweat."

Elysium [eh–LIZH-ee-um]: Underworld region of eternal sunshine and endless apple orchards where ghosts of heroes and of those who were good in life party on.

Furies [FYOOR-eez]: three winged immortals with red eyes and serpents for hair who pursue and punish wrongdoers, especially children who insult their mothers; their full names are **Tisiphone** [ti-Z-fun-ee), **Megaera** [MEG-ah-rah], and **Alecto** [Eal-ECK-toe], but around my palace, they're known as Tisi, Meg, and Alec.

Gaia [GUY-uh]: Mother Earth, married to Uranus, Father Sky; mom to the Titans, Cyclopes, Hundred-Handed Ones, Typhon, and other giant monsters, and granny to us Olympian gods.

Hades [HEY-deez]: Ruler of the Underworld, Lord of the Dead, King Hades, that's me. I'm also god of Wealth, owner of all the gold, silver, and precious jewels in the earth. The Romans call me **Pluto**.

Helios [HEE-lee-ohss]: the Titan sun god; drives his fiery chariot from east to west across the sky each day; son of Hyperion.

Hephaestus [huh-FESS-tus]: lame god of the forge, metalworkers, jewelers, and blacksmiths. The Romans call him **Vulcan**.

Hera [HERE-uh]: my sister, Queen of the Olympians, goddess of marriage. The Romans call her **Juno**. I call her the Boss.

Hermes [HER-meez]: god of shepherds, travelers, inventors, merchants, business executives, gamblers, and thieves; messenger of the gods; escorts the ghosts of dead mortals down to the Underworld. The Romans call him **Mercury**.

Hestia [HESS-tee-uh]: my sister; goddess of the hearth; a real homebody. The Romans call her **Vesta.**

Hundred-Handed Ones: three oddball brothers— Fingers, Highfive, and Lefty—who each have fifty heads and one hundred hands; brothers of the Cyclopes and the Titans.

Hyperion [hi-PEER-ee-un]: a way-cool Titan dude,

once in charge of the sun and all the light in the universe. Now retired, he owns a cattle ranch in the Underworld. Has a taste for good books.

Hypnos [HIP-nohss]: god of sleep; brother of Thanatos; son of Nyx, or night. Shhh! he's napping.

ichor [EYE-ker]: god blood.

immortal: a being, such as a god or possibly a monster, who will never die—like me.

Medusa [meh-DOO-suh]: one of three Gorgons, with snakes for hair.

Meg: see **Furies**.

mortal: a being who one day must die; I hate to be the one to break this to you, but *you* are a mortal.

Mount Olympus [oh-LIM-pess]: the highest mountain in Greece; its peak is home to all the major gods, except for my brother, Po, and me.

nectar [NECK-ter]: what we gods like to drink; has properties that invigorate us and make us look good and feel godly.

Pan: god of woods, fields, and mountains; has a goat's horns, ears, legs, tail, and a goatee; his earsplitting yell can create a wild fear known as "panic."

Persephone [per-SEF-uh-nee]: goddess of spring and Queen of the Underworld. The Romans call her **Proserpina**.

pomegranate [POM-uh-gran-it]: a fruit with red rind and juicy red pulp full of seeds.

Pool of Lethe [LEE-thee]: also called the Pool of Forgetfulness. Underworld watering hole for common ghosts; drinking its waters makes the ghosts forget their lives on earth.

Pool of Memory: Underworld pool where ghosts-in-the-know meet for drinks and to exchange memories.

Poseidon [po-SIGH-dun]: my bro Po; god of the seas, rivers, lakes, and earthquakes; claims to have invented horses as well as the doggie paddle. The Romans call him **Neptune.**

Rhea [REE-uh]: Titaness, wife of Cronus, and mom to Po, Hestia, Demeter, Hera, Zeus, and me, Hades.

Roman numerals: what the ancients used instead of counting on their fingers. Makes you glad you live in the age of Arabic numerals and calculators, doesn't it?

I	1	XI	11	XXX	30
II	2	XII	12	XL	40
III	3	XIII	13	L	50
IV	4	XIV	14	LX	60
V	5	XV	15	LXX	70
VI	6	XVI	16	LXXX	80
VII	7	XVII	17	XC	90
VIII	8	XVIII	18	C	100
IX	9	XIX	19	D	500
X	10	XX	20	M	1000

Tartarus [TAR-tar-us]: the deepest pit in the Underworld and home of the Punishment Fields, where burning flames and red-hot lava eternally torment the ghosts of the wicked.

Thanatos [THAN-uh-toss]: god of death; brother of Hypnos.

Tisi: see **Furies**.

Underworld: my very own kingdom, where the ghosts of dead mortals come to spend eternity.

Zeus [ZOOSE]: rhymes with *goose*, which pretty much says it all; last, and definitely least, my little brother, a major myth-o-maniac and a cheater, who managed to set himself up as Ruler of the Universe. The Romans call him **Jupiter.**

Kate McMullan is the author of more than fifty books for children, including several collaborations with her husband, noted illustrator Jim McMullan. Their latest, *I Stink!*, stars a garbage truck with attitude.

Kate and her husband live in New York City and Sag Harbor with their daughter and their two mewses, George and Wendy.

Visit Kate at www.katemcmullan.com